The Christmas Story Book

The Christmas Story Book

The Neumann Press
Long Prairie, Minnesota 56347

Table of Contents

The Christmas Story

And it came to pass that in those days there went out a decree from Caesar Augustus, that the whole world should be enrolled. This enrolling was first made by Cyrinus, the governor of Syria. And all went to be enrolled, every one into his own city. And Joseph also went up from Galilee, out of the city of Nazareth into Judea, to the city of David, which is called Bethlehem: because he was of the house and family of David, to be enrolled with Mary his espoused wife, who was with child.

And it came to pass, that when they were there, her days were accomplished, that she should be delivered. And she brought forth her first-born son, and wrapped him up in swaddling clothes, and laid him in a manger; because there was no room for them in the inn.

And there were in the same country shepherds watching, and keeping the night-watches over their flock. And behold an angel of the Lord stood by them, and the brightness of God shone round about them, and they feared with a great fear. And the angel said to them: Fear not; for, behold, I bring you good tidings of great joy, that shall be to all the people; for this day is born to you a Saviour, who is Christ the Lord, in the city of David. And this shall be a sign unto you: You shall find the infant wrapped in swaddling clothes, and laid in a manger. And suddenly there was with the angel a multitude of the heavenly army, praising God, and saying: Glory to God in the highest; and on earth peace to men of good will.

And it came to pass, after the angels departed from them into heaven, the shepherds said one to another: Let us go over to Bethlehem, and let us see this word that is come to pass, which the Lord hath shewed to us. And they came with haste; and they found Mary and Joseph, and the infant lying in the manger. And seeing, they understood of the word that had been spoken to them concerning this child. And all that heard, wondered; and at those things that were told them by the shepherds. But Mary kept all these words, pondering them in her heart. And the shepherds returned, glorifying and praising God, for all the things they had heard and seen, as it was told unto them.

The Legend of the Christmas Rose

by SELMA LAGERLÖF

ROBBER MOTHER, who lived in Robbers' Cave up in Göinge forest, went down to the village one day on a begging tour. Robber Father, who was an outlawed man, did not dare to leave the forest. She took with her five youngsters, and each youngster bore a sack on his back as long as himself. When Robber Mother stepped inside the door of a cabin, no one dared refuse to give her whatever she demanded; for she was not above coming back the following night and setting fire to the house if she had not been well received. Robber Mother and her brood were worse than a pack of wolves, and many a man felt like running a spear through them; but it was never done, because they all knew that the man stayed up in the forest, and he would have known how to wreak vengeance if anything had happened to the children or the old woman.

Now that Robber Mother went from house to house and begged, she came to Övid, which at that time was a cloister. She rang the bell of the cloister gate and asked for food. The watchman let down a small wicket in the gate and handed her six round bread cakes—one for herself and one for each of the five children.

While the mother was standing quietly at the gate, her youngsters were running about. And now one of them came and pulled at her skirt, as a signal that he had discovered something which she ought to come and see, and Robber Mother followed him promptly.

The entire cloister was surrounded by a high and strong wall, but the youngster had managed to find a little back gate which stood ajar. When Robber Mother got there, she pushed the gate open and walked inside without asking leave, as it was her custom to do.

Övid Cloister was managed at that time by Abbot Hans, who knew all about herbs. Just within the cloister wall he had planted a little herb garden, and it was into this that the old woman had forced her way.

At first glance Robber Mother was so astonished that she paused at the gate. It was high summertide, and Abbot Hans' garden was so full of flowers that the eyes were fairly dazzled by the blues, reds, and yellows, as one looked into it. But presently an indulgent smile spread over her features, and she started to walk up a narrow path that lay between many flowerbeds.

In the garden a lay brother walked about, pulling up weeds. It was he who had left the door in the wall open, that he might throw the weeds and tares on the rubbish heap outside.

When he saw Robber Mother coming in, with all five youngsters in tow, he ran toward her at once and ordered them away. But the beggar woman walked right on as before. The lay brother knew of no other remedy than to run into the cloister and call for help.

He returned with two stalwart monks, and Robber Mother saw that now it meant business! She let out a perfect volley of shrieks, and, throwing herself upon the monks, clawed and bit at them; so did all the youngsters.

The men soon learned that she could overpower them, and all they could do was to go back into the cloister for reinforcements.

As they ran through the passage-way which led to the cloister, they met Abbot Hans, who came rushing out to learn what all this noise was about.

He upbraided them for using force and forbade their calling for help. He sent both monks back to their work, and although he was an old and fragile man, he took with him only the lay brother.

He came up to the woman and asked in a mild tone if the garden pleased her.

Robber Mother turned defiantly toward Abbot Hans, for she expected only to be trapped and overpowered. But when she noticed his white hair and bent form, she answered peaceably, "First, when I saw this, I thought I had never seen a prettier garden; but now I see that it can't be compared with one I know of. If you could see the garden of which I am thinking you would uproot all the flowers planted here and cast them away like weeds."

The Abbot's assistant was hardly less proud of the flowers than the Abbot himself, and after hearing her remarks he laughed derisively.

Robber Mother grew crimson with rage to think that her word was doubted, and she cried out: "You monks, who are holy men, certainly must know that on every Christmas Eve the great Göinge forest is transformed into a beautiful garden, to commemorate the hour of our Lord's birth. We who live in the forest have seen this happen every year. And in that garden I have seen flowers so lovely that I dared not lift my hand to pluck them."

Ever since his childhood, Abbot Hans had heard it said that on every Christmas Eve the forest was dressed in holiday glory. He had often longed to see it, but he had never had the good fortune. Eagerly he begged and implored Robber Mother that he might come up to the Robbers' Cave on Christmas Eve. If she would only send one of her children to show him the way, he could ride up there alone, and he would never betray them—on the contrary, he would reward them insofar as it lay in his power.

Robber Mother said no at first, for she was thinking of Robber Father and of the peril which might befall him should she permit Abbot Hans to ride up to their cave. At the same time the desire to prove to the monk that the garden which she knew was more beautiful than his got the better of her, and she gave in.

"But more than one follower you cannot take with you," said she, "and you are not to waylay us or trap us, as sure as you are a holy man."

This Abbot Hans promised, and then Robber Mother went her way.

It happened that Archbishop Absalon from Lund came to Övid and remained through the night. The lay brother heard Abbot Hans telling the Bishop about Robber Father and asking him for a letter of ransom for the man, that he might lead an honest life among respectable folk.

But the Archbishop replied that he did not care to let the robber loose among honest folk in the villages. It would be best for all that he remain in the forest.

Then Abbot Hans grew zealous and told the Bishop all about Göinge forest, which, every year at Yuletide, clothed itself in summer bloom around the Robbers' Cave. "If these bandits are not so bad but that God's glories can be made manifest to them, surely we cannot be too wicked to experience the same blessing."

The Archbishop knew how to answer Abbot Hans. "This much I will promise you, Abbot Hans," he said, smiling, "that any day you send me a blossom from the garden in Göinge forest, I will give you letters of ransom for all the outlaws you may choose to plead for."

The following Christmas Eve Abbot Hans was on his way to the forest. One of Robber Mother's wild youngsters ran ahead of him, and close behind him was the lay brother.

It turned out to be a long and hazardous ride. They climbed steep and slippery side paths, crawled over swamp and marsh, and pushed through windfall and bramble. Just as daylight was waning, the robber boy guided them across a forest meadow, skirted by tall, naked leaf trees and green fir trees. Back of the meadow loomed a mountain wall, and in this wall they saw a door of thick boards. Now Abbot Hans understood that they had arrived, and dismounted. The child opened the heavy door for him, and he looked into a poor mountain grotto, with bare stone walls. Robber Mother was seated before a log fire that burned in the middle of the floor. Alongside the walls were beds of virgin pine and moss, and on one of these beds lay Robber Father asleep.

"Come in, you out there!" shouted Robber Mother without rising, "and fetch the horses in with you, so they won't be destroyed by the night cold."

Abbot Hans walked boldly into the cave, and the lay brother followed. Here were wretchedness and poverty! and nothing was done to celebrate Christmas.

Robber Mother spoke in a tone as haughty and dictatorial as any well-to-do peasant woman. "Sit down by the fire and warm yourself, Abbot Hans," said she; "and if you have food with you, eat, for the food which we in the forest prepare you wouldn't care to taste. And if you are tired after the long journey, you can lie down on one of these beds to sleep. You needn't be afraid of oversleeping, for I'm sitting here by the fire keeping watch. I shall awaken you in time to see that which you have come up here to see."

Abbot Hans obeyed Robber Mother and brought forth his food sack; but he was so fatigued after the journey he was hardly able to eat, and as soon as he could stretch himself on the bed, he fell asleep.

The lay brother was also assigned a bed to rest and he dropped into a doze.

When he woke up, he saw that Abbot Hans had left his bed and was sitting by the fire talking with Robber Mother. The outlawed robber sat also by the fire. He was a tall, raw-boned man with a dull, sluggish appearance. His back was turned to Abbot Hans, as though he would have it appear that he was not listening to the conversation.

Abbot Hans was telling Robber Mother all about the Christmas preparations he had seen on the journey, reminding her of Christmas feasts and games which she must have known in her youth, when she lived at peace with mankind.

At first Robber Mother answered in short, gruff sentences, but by degrees she became more subdued and listened more intently. Suddenly Robber Father turned toward Abbot Hans and shook his clenched fist in his face. "You miserable monk! Did you come here to coax from me my wife and children? Don't you know that I am an outlaw and may not leave the forest?"

Abbot Hans looked him fearlessly in the eyes. "It is my purpose to get a letter of ransom for you from Archbishop Absalson," said he. He had hardly finished speaking when the robber and his wife burst out laughing. They knew well enough the kind of mercy a forest robber could expect from Bishop Absalon!

"Oh, if I get a letter of ransom from Absolon," said Robber Father, "then I'll promise you that never again will I steal so much as a goose."

Suddenly Robber Mother rose. "You sit here and talk, Abbot Hans," she said, "so that we are forgetting to look at the forest. Now I can hear, even in this cave, how the Christmas bells are ringing."

The words were barely uttered when they all sprang up and rushed out. But in the forest it was still dark night and bleak winter. The only thing they marked was a distant clang borne on a light south wind.

When the bells had been ringing a few moments, a sudden illumination penetrated the forest; the next moment it was dark again, and then light came back. It pushed its way forward between the stark trees, like a shimmering mist. The darkness merged into a faint daybreak. Then Abbot Hans saw that the snow had vanished from the ground, as if someone had removed a carpet, and the earth began to take on a green covering. The moss-tufts thickened and raised themselves, and the spring blossoms shot upward their swelling buds, which already had a touch of color.

Again it grew hazy; but almost immediately there came a new wave of light. Then the leaves of the trees burst into bloom, crossbeaks hopped from branch to branch, and the woodpeckers hammered on the limbs until the splinters fairly flew around them. A flock of starlings from up country lighted in a fir top to rest.

When the next warm wind came along, the blueberries ripened and the baby squirrels began playing on the branches of the trees.

The next light wave that came rushing in brought with it the scent of newly ploughed acres. Pine and spruce trees were so thickly clothed with red cones that they shone like crimson mantles and forest flowers covered the ground till it was all red, blue, and yellow.

Abbot Hans bent down to the earth and broke off a wild strawberry blossom, and, as he straightened up, the berry ripened in his hand.

The mother fox came out of her lair with a big litter of black-legged young. She went up to Robber Mother and scratched at her skirt, and Robber Mother bent down to her and praised her young.

Robber Mother's youngsters let out perfect shrieks of delight. They stuffed themselves with wild strawberries that hung on the bushes. One of them played with a litter of young hares; another ran a race with some young crows, which had hopped from their nest before they were really ready.

Robber Father was standing out on a marsh eating raspberries. When he glanced up, a big black bear stood beside him. Robber Father broke off a twig and struck the bear on the nose. "Keep to your own ground, you!" he said; "this is my turf." The huge bear turned around and lumbered off in another direction.

Then all the flowers whose seeds had been brought from foreign lands began to blossom. The loveliest roses climbed up the mountain wall in a race with the blackberry vines, and from the forest meadow sprang flowers as large as human faces.

Abbot Hans thought of the flower he was to pluck for Bishop Absalon; but each new flower that appeared was more beautiful than the others, and he wanted to choose the most beautiful of all.

Then Abbot Hans marked how all grew still; the birds hushed their songs, the flowers ceased growing, and the young foxes played no more. From far in the distance faint harp tones were heard, and celestial song, like a soft murmur, reached him.

He clasped his hands and dropped to his knees. His face was radiant with bliss.

But beside Abbot Hans stood the lay brother who had accompanied him. In his mind there were dark thoughts. "This cannot be a true miracle," he thought, "since it is revealed to malefactors. This does not come from God, but is sent hither by Satan. It is the Evil One's power that is tempting us and compelling us to see that which has no real existence."

The angel throng was so near now that Abbot Hans saw their bright forms through the forest branches. The lay brother saw them, too; but back of all this wondrous beauty he saw only some dread evil.

All the while birds had been circling around the head of Abbot Hans, and they let him take them in his hands. But all the animals were afraid of the lay brother; no bird perched on his shoulder, no snake played at his feet. Then there came a little forest dove. When she marked that the angels were nearing, she plucked up courage and flew down on the lay brother's shoulder and laid her head against his cheek.

Then it appeared to him as if sorcery were come right upon him, to tempt and corrupt him. He struck with his hand at the forest dove and cried in such a loud voice that it rang thoughout the forest, "Go thou back to hell, whence thou art come!"

Just then the angels were so near that Abbot Hans felt the feathery touch of their great wings, and he bowed down to earth in reverent greeting.

But when the lay brother's words sounded, their song was hushed and the holy guests turned in flight. At the same time the light and the mild warmth vanished in unspeakable terror for the darkness and cold in a human heart. Darkness sank over the earth, like a coverlet; frost came, all the growths shrivelled up; the animals and birds hastened away; the leaves dropped from the trees, rustling like rain.

Abbot Hans felt how his heart, which had but lately swelled with bliss, was now contracting with insufferable agony. "I can never outlive this," thought he, "that the angels from heaven had been so close to me and were driven away; that they wanted to sing Chrismas carols for me and were driven to flight."

Then he remembered the flower he had promised Bishop Absalon, and at the last moment he fumbled among the leaves and moss to try and find a blossom. But he sensed how the ground under his fingers froze and how the white snow came gliding over the ground. Then his heart caused him even greater anguish. He could not rise, but fell prostrate on the ground and lay there.

When the robber fold and the lay brother had groped their way back to the cave, they missed Abbot Hans. They took brands with them and went out to search for him. They found him dead upon the coverlet of snow.

When Abbot Hans had been carried down to Övid, those who took charge of the dead saw that he held his right hand locked tight around something which he must have grasped at the moment of death. When they finally got his hand open, they found that the thing which he had held in such an iron grip was a pair of white root bulbs, which he had torn from among the moss and leaves.

When the lay brother who had accompanied Abbot Hans saw the bulbs, he took them and planted them in Abbot Hans' herb garden.

He guarded them the whole year to see if any flower would spring from them. But in vain he waited through the spring, the summer, and the autumn. Finally, when winter had set in and all the leaves and the flowers were dead, he ceased caring for them.

But when Christmas Eve came again, he was so strongly reminded of Abbot Hans that he wandered out into the garden to think of him. And look! as he came to the spot where he had planted the bare root bulbs, he saw that from them had sprung flourishing green stalks, which bore beautiful flowers with silver white leaves.

He called out all the monks at Övid, and when they saw that this plant bloomed on Christmas Eve, when all the other growths were as if dead, they understood that this flower had in truth been plucked by Abbot Hans from the Christmas garden in Göinge forest. Then the lay brother asked the monks if he might take a few blossoms to Bishop Absalon.

When Bishop Absalon beheld the flowers, which had sprung from the earth in darkest winter, he turned as pale as if he had met a ghost. He sat in silence a moment; thereupon he said, "Abbot Hans has faithfully kept his word and I shall also keep mine."

He handed the letter of ransom to the lay brother, who departed at once for the Robbers' Cave. When he stepped in there on Christmas Day, the robber came toward him with axe uplifted. "I'd like to hack you monks into bits, as many as you are!" said he. "It must be your fault that Göinge forest did not last night dress itself in Christmas bloom."

"The fault is mine alone," said the lay brother, "and I will gladly die for it; but first I must deliver a message from Abbot Hans." And he drew forth the Bishop's letter and told the man that he was free.

Robber Father stood there pale and speechless, but Robber Mother said in his name, "Abbot Hans has indeed kept his word, and Robber Father will keep his."

When the robber and his wife left the cave, the lay brother moved in and lived all alone in the forest, in constant meditation and prayer that his hard-heartedness might be forgiven him.

But Göinge forest never again celebrated the hour of our Saviour's birth; and of all its glory, there lives today only the plant which Abbot Hans had plucked. It has been named CHRISTMAS ROSE. And each year at Christmastide she sends forth from the earth her green stalks and white blossoms, as if she never could forget that she had once grown in the great Christmas garden at Göinge forest.

A Christmas Mystery

The Story of Three Wise Men

by WILLIAM J. LOCKE

THREE men who had gained great fame and honor throughout the world met unexpectedly in front of the bookstall at Paddington Station. Like most of the great ones of the earth they were personally acquainted, and they exchanged surprised greetings.

Sir Angus McCurdie, the eminent physicist, scowled at the two others beneath his heavy black eyebrows.

"I'm going to a God-forsaken place in Cornwall called Trehenna," said he.

"That's odd; so am I," croaked Professor Biggleswade. He was a little, untidy man with round spectacles, a fringe of greyish beard and a weak, rasping voice, and he knew more of Assyriology than any man, living or dead. A flippant pupil once remarked that the Professor's face was furnished with a Babylonic cuneiform in lieu of features.

"People called Deverill, at Foullis Castle?" asked Sir Angus.

"Yes," replied Professor Biggleswade.

"How curious! I am going to the Deverills, too," said the third man.

This man was the Right Honorable Viscount Doyne, the renowned Empire Builder and Administrator, around whose solitary and remote life popular imagination had woven many legends. He looked at the world through tired grey eyes, and the heavy, drooping, blonde moustache seemed tired, too, and had dragged down the tired face into deep furrows. He was smoking a long black cigar.

"I suppose we may as well travel down together," said Sir Angus, not very cordially.

Lord Doyne said courteously: "I have a reserved carriage. The railway company is always good enough to place one at my disposal. It would give me great pleasure if you would share it."

The invitation was accepted, and the three men crossed the busy, crowded platform to take their seats in the great express train. A porter, laden with an incredible load of paraphernalia, trying to make his way through the press, happened to jostle Sir Angus McCurdie. He rubbed his shoulder fretfully.

"Why the whole land should be turned into a beer garden on account of this exploded superstition of Christmas is one of the anomalies of modern civilization. Look at this insensate welter of fools traveling in wild herds to disgusting places merely because it's Christmas!"

"You seem to be traveling yourself, McCurdie," said Lord Doyne.

"Yes—and why the devil I'm doing it, I've not the faintest notion," replied Sir Angus.

"It's going to be a beast of a journey," he remarked some moments later, as the train carried them slowly out of the station. "The whole country is under snow—and as far as I can understand we have to change twice and wind up with a twenty-mile motor drive."

He was an iron-faced, beetle-browed, stern man, and this morning he did not seem to be in the best of tempers.

Finding his companions inclined to be sympathetic, he continued his lamentation.

"And merely because it's Christmas I've had to shut up my laboratory and give my young fools a holiday—just when I was in the midst of a most important series of experiments."

Professor Biggleswade, who had heard vaguely of and rather looked down upon such new-fangled toys as radium and thorium and helium and argon—for the latest astonishing developments in the theory of radio-activity had brought Sir Angus McCurdie his world-wide fame—said somewhat ironically:

"If the experiments were so important, why didn't you lock yourself up with your test tubes and electric batteries and finish them alone?"

"Man!" said McCurdie, bending across the carriage, and speaking with a curious intensity of voice, "d'ye know I'd give a hundred pounds to be able to answer that question?"

"What do you mean?" asked the Professor, startled.

"I should like to know why I'm sitting in this d——d train and going to visit a couple of addle-headed society people whom I'm scarcely acquainted with, when I might be at home in my own good company furthering the progress of science."

"I myself," said the Professor, "am not acquainted with them at all."

It was Sir Angus McCurdie's turn to look surprised.

"Then why are you spending Christmas with them?"

"I reviewed a ridiculous blank-verse tragedy written by Deverill on the Death of Sennacherib. Historically it was puerile. I said so in no measured terms. He wrote a letter claiming to be a poet and not an archaeologist. I replied that the day had passed when poets could with impunity commit the abominable crime of distorting history. He retorted with some futile argument, and we went on exchanging letters, until his invitation and my acceptance concluded the correspondence."

McCurdie, still bending his black brows on him, asked him why he had not declined. The Professor screwed up his face till it looked more like a cuneiform than ever. He, too, found the question difficult to answer, but he showed a bold front.

"I felt it my duty," said he, "to teach that preposterous ignoramus something worth knowing about Sennacherib. Besides I am a bachelor and would sooner spend Christmas, as to whose irritating and meaningless annoyance I cordially agree with you, among strangers than among my married sisters' numerous and nerve-racking families."

Sir Angus McCurdie, the hard, metallic apostle of radioactivity, glanced for a moment out of the window at the grey, frost-bitten fields. Then he said:

"I'm a widower. My wife died many years ago and, thank God, we had no children. I generally spend Christmas alone."

He looked out of the window again. Professor Biggleswade suddenly remembered the popular story of the great scientist's antecedents, and reflected that as McCurdie had once run, a barefoot urchin, through the Glasgow mud, he was likely to have little kith or kin. He himself envied McCurdie. He was always praying to be delivered from his sisters and nephews and nieces, whose embarrassing demands no calculated coldness could repress.

"Children are the root of all evil," said he. "Happy the man who has his quiver empty."

Sir Angus McCurdie did not reply at once; when he spoke again it was with reference to their prospective host.

"I met Deverill," said he, "at the Royal Society's Soirée this year. One of my assistants was demonstrating a peculiar property of thorium and Deverill seemed interested. I asked him to come to my laboratory the next day, and found he didn't know a d—d thing about anything. That's all the acquaintance I have with him."

Lord Doyne, the great administrator, who had been wearily turning over the pages of an illustrated weekly chiefly filled with flamboyant photographs of obscure actresses, took his gold glasses from his nose and the black cigar from his lips, and addressed his companions.

"I've been considerably interested in your conversation," said he, "and as you've been frank, I'll be frank too. I knew Mrs. Deverill's mother, Lady Carstairs, very well years ago, and of course Mrs. Deverill when she was a child. Deverill I came across once in Egypt—he had been sent on a diplomatic mission to Teheran. As for our being invited on such slight acquaintance, little Mrs. Deverill has the reputation of being the only really successful celebrity hunter in England. She inherited the faculty from her mother, who entertained the whole world. We're sure to find archbishops, and eminent actors, and illustrious divorcées asked to meet us. That's one thing. But why I, who loathe country house parties and children and Christmas as much as Biggleswade, am going down there to-day, I can no more explain than you can. It's a devilish odd coincidence."

The three men looked at one another. Suddenly McCurdie shivered and drew his fur coat around him.

"I'll thank you," said he, "to shut that window."

"It is shut," said Doyne.

"It's just uncanny," said McCurdie, looking from one to the other.

"What?" asked Doyne.

"Nothing, if you didn't feel it."

"There did seem to be a sudden draft," said Professor Biggleswade. "But as both window and door are shut, it could only be imaginary."

"It wasn't imaginary," muttered McCurdie.

Then he laughed harshly. "My father and mother came from Cromarty," he said with apparent irrelevance.

"That's the Highlands," said the Professor.

"Ay," said McCurdie.

Lord Doyne said nothing, but tugged at his moustache and looked out of the window as the frozen meadows and bits of river and willows raced past. A dead silence fell on them. McCurdie broke it with another laugh and took a whiskey flask from his hand-bag.

"Have a nip?"

"Thanks, no," said the Professor. "I have to keep to a strict dietary, and I only drink hot milk and water—and of that sparingly. I have some in a thermos bottle."

Lord Doyne also declining the whiskey, McCurdie swallowed a dram and declared himself to be better. The Professor took from his bag a foreign review in which a German sciolist had dared to question his interpretation of a Hittite inscription. Over the man's ineptitude he fell asleep and snored loudly.

To escape from his immediate neighborhood McCurdie went to the other end of the seat and faced Lord Doyne, who had resumed his gold glasses and his listless contemplation of obscure actresses. McCurdie lit a pipe, Doyne another black cigar. The train thundered on.

Presently they all lunched together in the restaurant car. The windows steamed, but here and there through a wiped patch of pane a white world was revealed. The snow was falling. As they passed through Westbury, McCurdie looked mechanically for the famous white horse carved into the chalk of the down; but it was not visible beneath the thick covering of snow.

"It'll be just like this all the way to Gehenna—Trehenna, I mean," said McCurdie.

Doyne nodded. He had done his life's work amid all extreme fiercenesses of heat and cold, in burning droughts, in simoons, and in icy wildernesses, and a ray or two more of the pale sun or a flake or two more of the gentle snow of England mattered to him but little. But Biggleswade rubbed the pane with his table-napkin and gazed apprehensively at the prospect.

"If only this wretched train would stop," said he, "I would go back again."

And he thought how comfortable it would be to sneak home again to his books and thus elude not only the Deverills, but the Christmas jollities of his sisters' families, who would think him miles away. But the train was timed not to stop till Plymouth, two hundred and thirty-five miles from London, and thither was he being relentlessly carried. Then he quarrelled with his food, which brought a certain consolation.

* * * * * *

The train did stop, however, before Plymouth—indeed, before Exeter. An accident on the line had dislocated the traffic. The express was held up for an hour, and when it was permitted to proceed, instead of thundering on, it went cautiously, subject to continual stoppings. It arrived at Plymouth two hours late. The travelers learned that they had missed the connection on which they had counted and that they could not reach Trehenna till nearly ten o'clock. After weary waiting at Plymouth they took their seats in the little, cold local train that was to carry them another stage on their journey. Hot-water cans put in at Plymouth mitigated to some extent the iciness of the compartment. But that only lasted a comparatively short time, for soon they were set down at a desolate, shelterless wayside junction, dumped in the midst of a hilly snow-covered waste, where they went through another weary wait for another dismal local train that was to carry them to Trehenna. And in this train there were no hot-water cans, so that the compartment was as cold as death. McCurdie fretted and shook his fist in the direction of Trehenna.

"And when we get there we have still a twenty miles' motor drive to Foullis Castle. It's a fool name and we're fools to be going there."

"I shall die of bronchitis," wailed Professor Biggleswade.

"A man dies when it is appointed for him to die," said Lord Doyne, in his tired way; and he went on smoking long black cigars.

"It's not the dying that worries me," said McCurdie. "That's a mere mechanical process which every organic being from a king to a cauliflower has to pass through. It's the being forced against my will and my reason to come on this accursed journey, which something tells me will become more and more accursed as we go on, that is driving me to distraction."

"What will be, will be," said Doyne.

"I can't see where the comfort of that reflection comes in," said Biggleswade.

"And yet you've traveled in the East," said Doyne. "I suppose you know the Valley of the Tigris as well as any man living."

"Yes," said the Professor. "I can say I dug my way from Tekrit to Bagdad and left not a stone unexamined."

"Perhaps, after all," Doyne remarked, "that's not quite the way to know the East."

"I never wanted to know the modern East," returned the Professor. "What is there in it of interest compared with the mighty civilizations that have gone before?"

McCurdie took a pull from his flask.

"I'm glad I thought of having a refill at Plymouth," said he.

At last, after many stops at little lonely stations they arrived at Trehenna. The guard opened the door and they stepped out on to the snow-covered platform. An oil lamp hung from the tiny pent-house roof that, structurally, was Trehenna Station. They looked around at the silent gloom of white undulating moorland, and it seemed a place where no man lived and only ghosts could have a bleak and unsheltered being. A porter came up and helped the guard with the luggage. Then they realized that the station was built on a small embankment, for, looking over the railing, they saw below the two great lamps of a motor-car. A fur-clad chauffeur met them at the bottom of the stairs. He clapped his hands together and informed them cheerily that he had been waiting for four hours. It was the bitterest winter in these parts within the memory of man, said he, and he himself had not seen snow there for five years. Then he settled the three travelers in the great roomy touring car covered with a Cape-cart hood, wrapped them up in many rugs and started.

After a few moments, the huddling together of their bodies—for, the Professor being a spare man, there was room for them all on the back seat—the pile of rugs, the serviceable and all but air-tight hood, induced a pleasant warmth and a pleasant drowsiness. Where they were being driven they knew not. The perfectly upholstered seat eased their limbs, the easy swinging motion of the car soothed their spirits. They felt that already they had reached the luxuriously appointed home which, after all, they knew awaited them. McCurdie no longer railed, Professor Biggleswade forgot the dangers of bronchitis, and Lord Doyne twisted the stump of a black cigar between his lips without any desire to relight it. A tiny electric lamp inside the hood made the darkness of the world to right and left and in front of the talc windows still darker. McCurdie and Biggleswade fell into a doze. Lord Doyne chewed the end of his cigar. The car sped on through an unseen wilderness.

Suddenly there was a horrid jolt and a lurch and a leap and a rebound, and then the car stood still, quivering like a ship that has been struck by a heavy sea. The three men were pitched and tossed and thrown sprawling over one another onto the bottom of the car. Biggleswade screamed. McCurdie cursed. Doyne scrambled from the confusion of rugs and limbs and, tearing open the side of the Cape-cart hood, jumped out. The chauffeur had also just leaped from his seat. It was pitch dark save for the great shaft of light down the snowy road cast by the acetylene lamps. The snow had ceased falling.

"What's gone wrong?"

"It sounds like the axle," said the chauffeur ruefully.

He unshipped a lamp and examined the car, which had wedged itself against a great drift of snow on the off side. Meanwhile McCurdie and Biggleswade had alighted.

"Yes, it's the axle," said the chauffeur.

"Then we're done," remarked Doyne.

"I'm afraid so, my lord."

"What's the matter? Can't we get on?" asked Biggleswade in his querulous voice.

McCurdie laughed. "How can we get on with a broken axle? The thing's as useless as a man with a broken back. Gad, I was right. I said it was going to be an infernal journey."

The little Professor wrung his hands. "But what's to be done?" he cried.

"Tramp it," said Lord Doyne, lighting a fresh cigar.

"It's ten miles," said the chauffeur.

"It would be the death of me," the Professor wailed.

"I utterly refuse to walk ten miles through a Polar waste with a gouty foot," McCurdie declared wrathfully.

The chauffeur offered a solution of the difficulty. He would set out alone for Foullis Castle—five miles farther on was an inn where he could obtain a horse and trap—and would return for the three gentlemen with another car. In the meanwhile they could take shelter in a little house which they had just passed, some half mile up the road. This was agreed to. The chauffeur went on cheerily enough with a lamp, and the three travelers with another lamp started off in the opposite direction. As far as they could see they were in a long, desolate valley, a sort of No Man's Land, deathly silent. The eastern sky had cleared somewhat, and they faced a loose rack through which one pale star was dimly visible.

* * * * * *

"I'm a man of science," said McCurdie as they trudged through the snow, "and I dismiss the supernatural as contrary to reason; but I have Highland blood in my veins that plays me exasperating tricks. My reason tells me that this place is only a commonplace moor, yet it seems like a Valley of Bones haunted by malignant spirits who have lured us here to our destruction. There's something guiding us now. It's just uncanny."

"Why on earth did we ever come?" croaked Biggleswade.

Lord Doyne answered: "The Koran says, 'Nothing can befall us but what God hath destined for us.' So why worry?"

"Because I'm not a Mohammedan," retorted Biggleswade.

"You might be worse," said Doyne.

Presently the dim outline of the little house grew perceptible. A faint light shone from the window. It stood unfenced by any kind of hedge or railing a few feet away from the road in a little hollow beneath some rising ground. As far as they could discern in the darkness when they drew near, the house was a mean, dilapidated hovel. A guttering candle stood on the inner sill of the small window and afforded a vague view into a mean interior. Doyne held up the lamp so that its rays fell full on the door. As he did so, an exclamation broke from his lips and he hurried forward, followed by the others. A man's body lay huddled together on the snow by the threshold. He was dressed like a peasant, in old corduroy trousers and rough coat, and a handkerchief was knotted round his neck. In his hand he grasped the neck of a broken bottle. Doyne set the lamp on the ground and the three bent down together over the man. Close by the neck lay the rest of the broken bottle, whose contents had evidently run out into the snow.

"Drunk?" asked Biggleswade.

Doyne felt the man and laid his hand on his heart.

"No," said he, "dead."

McCurdie leaped to his full height. "I told you the place was uncanny!" he cried. "It's fey." Then he hammered wildly at the door.

There was no response. He hammered again till it rattled. This time a faint prolonged sound like the wailing of a strange sea-creature was heard from within the house. McCurdie turned round, his teeth chattering.

"Did ye hear that, Doyne?"

"Perhaps it's a dog," said the Professor.

Lord Doyne, the man of action, pushed them aside and tried the door-handle. It yielded, the door stood open, and the gust of cold wind entering the house extinguished the candle within. They entered and found themselves in a miserable stone-paved kitchen, furnished with poverty-stricken meagreness—a wooden chair or two, a dirty table, some broken crockery, old cooking utensils, a fly-blown missionary society almanac, and a fireless grate. Doyne set the lamp on the table.

"We must bring him in," said he.

They returned to the threshold, and as they were bending over to grip the dead man the same sound filled the air, but this time louder, more intense, a cry of great agony. The sweat dripped from McCurdie's forehead. They lifted the dead man and brought him into the room, and after laying him on a dirty strip of carpet they did their best to straighten the stiff limbs. Biggleswade put on the table a bundle which he had picked up outside. It contained some poor provisions—a loaf, a piece of fat bacon, and a paper of tea. As far as they could guess (and as they learned later they guessed rightly) the man was the master of the house, who, coming home blind drunk from some distant inn, had fallen at his own threshold and got frozen to death. As they could not unclasp his fingers from the broken bottleneck they had to let him clutch it as a dead warrior clutches the hilt of his broken sword.

Then suddenly the whole place was rent with another and yet another long, soul-piercing moan of anguish.

"There's a second room," said Doyne, pointing to a door. "The sound comes from there."

He opened the door, peeped in, and then, returning for the lamp, disappeared, leaving McCurdie and Biggleswade in the pitch darkness, with the dead man on the floor.

"For heaven's sake, give me a drop of whiskey," said the Professor, "or I shall faint."

Presently the door opened and Lord Doyne appeared in the shaft of light. He beckoned to his companions.

"It is a woman in childbirth," he said in his even, tired voice. "We must aid her. She appears unconscious. Does either of you know anything about such things?"

They shook their heads, and the three looked at each other in dismay. Masters of knowledge that had won them world-wide fame and honor, they stood helpless, abashed before this, the commonest phenomenon of nature.

"My wife had no child," said McCurdie.

"I've avoided women all my life," said Biggleswade.

"And I've been too busy to think of them. God forgive me," said Doyne.

* * * * * *

The history of the next two hours was one that none of the three men ever cared to touch upon. They did things blindly, instinctively, as men do when they come face to face with the elemental. A fire was made, they knew not how, water drawn they knew not whence, and a kettle boiled. Doyne accustomed to command, directed. The others obeyed. At his suggestion they hastened to the wreck of the car and came staggering back beneath rugs and traveling bags which could supply clean linen and needful things, for amid the poverty of the house they could find nothing fit for human touch or use. Early they saw that the woman's strength was failing, and that she could not live. And there, in that nameless hovel, with death on the hearth-stone and death and life hovering over the pitiful bed, the three great men went through the pain and the horror and squalor of birth, and they knew that they had never yet stood before so great a mystery.

With the first wail of the newly born infant a last convulsive shudder passed through the frame of the unconscious mother. Then three or four short gasps for breath, and the spirit passed away. She was dead. Professor Biggleswade threw a corner of the sheet over her face, for he could not bear to see it.

They washed and dried the child as any crone of a midwife would have done, and dipped a small sponge which had always remained unused in a cut-glass bottle in Doyne's dressing-bag in the hot milk and water of Biggleswade's thermos bottle, and put it to his lips; and then they wrapped him up warm in some of their own woolen undergarments, and took him into the kitchen and placed him on a bed made of their fur coats in front of the fire. As the last piece of fuel was exhausted they took one of the wooden chairs and broke it up and cast it into the blaze. And then they raised the dead man from the strip of carpet and carried him into the bedroom and laid him reverently by the side of his dead wife, after which they left the dead in darkness and returned to the living. And the three grave men stood over the wisp of flesh that had been born a male into the world. Then, their task being accomplished, reaction came, and even Doyne, who had seen death in many lands, turned faint. But the others, losing control of their nerves, shook like men stricken with palsy.

Suddenly McCurdie cried in a high pitched voice, "My God! Don't you feel it?" and clutched Doyne by the arm. An expression of terror appeared on his iron features. "There! It's here with us."

Little Professor Biggleswade sat on a corner of the table and wiped his forehead.

"I heard it. I felt it. It was like the beating of wings."

"It's the fourth time," said McCurdie. "The first time was just before I accepted the Deverills' invitation. The second in the railway carriage this afternoon. The third on the way here. This is the fourth."

Biggleswade plucked nervously at the fringe of whisker under his jaws and said faintly, "It's the fourth time up to now. I thought it was fancy."

"I have felt it, too," said Doyne. "It is the Angel of Death." And he pointed to the room where the dead man and woman lay.

"For God's sake let us get away from this," cried Biggleswade.

"And leave the child to die, like the others?" said Doyne.

"We must see it through," said McCurdie.

A silence fell upon them as they sat round in the blaze with the new-born babe wrapped in its odd swaddling clothes asleep on the pile of fur coats, and it lasted until Sir Angus McCurdie looked at his watch.

"Good Lord," said he, "it's twelve o'clock."

"Christmas morning," said Biggleswade.

"A strange Christmas," mused Doyne.

McCurdie put up his hand. "There it is again! The beating of wings." And they listened like men spellbound. McCurdie kept his hand uplifted, and gazed over their heads at the wall, and his gaze was that of a man in a trance, and he spoke:

"Unto us a child is born, unto us a son is given—"

Doyne sprang from his chair, which fell behind him with a crash.

"Man—what the devil are you saying?"

Then McCurdie rose and met Biggleswade's eyes staring at him through the great round spectacles, and Biggleswade turned and met the eyes of Doyne. A pulsation like the beating of wings stirred the air.

The three wise men shivered with a queer exaltation. Something strange, mystical, dynamic had happened. It was as if scales had fallen from their eyes and they saw with a new vision. They stood together humbly, divested of all their greatness, touching one another in the instinctive fashion of children, as if seeking mutual protection, and they looked, with one accord, irresistibly compelled, at the child.

At last McCurdie unbent his black brows and said hoarsely:

"It was not the Angel of Death, Doyne, but another Messenger that drew us here."

The tiredness seemed to pass away from the great administrator's face, and he nodded his head with the calm of a man who has come to the quiet heart of a perplexing mystery.

"It's true," he murmured. "Unto us a child is born, unto us a son is given. Unto the three of us."

Biggleswade took off his great round spectacles and wiped them.

"Gaspar, Melchior, Balthazar. But where are the gold, frankincense and myrrh?"

"In our hearts, man," said McCurdie.

The babe cried and stretched its tiny limbs.

Instinctively they all knelt down together to discover, if possible, and administer ignorantly to, its wants. The scene had the appearance of an adoration.

* * * * * *

Then these three wise, lonely, childless men who, in furtherance of their own greatness, had cut themselves adrift from the sweet and simple things of life and from the kindly ways of their brethren, and had grown old in unhappy and profitless wisdom, knew that an inscrutable Providence had led them, as it had led three Wise Men of old, on a Christmas morning long ago, to a nativity which should give them a new wisdom, a new link with humanity, a new spiritual outlook, a new hope.

And, when their watch was ended, they wrapped up the babe with precious care, and carried him with them, an inalienable joy and possession, into the great world.

The Fir Tree

by HANS CHRISTIAN ANDERSEN

OUT in the forest stood a pretty little Fir Tree. It had a good place; it could have sunlight, air there was in plenty, and all around grew many larger comrades—pines as well as firs. But the little Fir Tree wished ardently to become greater. It did not care for the warm sun and the fresh air; it took no notice of the peasant children, who went about talking together, when they had come out to look for strawberries and raspberries. Often they came with a whole pot-full, or had strung berries on a straw; then they would sit down by the little Fir Tree and say, "How pretty and small that one is!" and the Tree did not like to hear that at all.

Next year he had grown a great joint, and the following year he was longer still, for in fir trees one can always tell by the number of rings they have how many years they have been growing.

"Oh, if I were only as great a tree as the others!" sighed the little Fir, "then I would spread my branches far around, and look out from my crown into the wide world. The birds would then build nests in my boughs, and when the wind blew I could nod just as grandly as the others yonder."

It took no pleasure in the sunshine, in the birds, and in the red clouds that went sailing over him morning and evening.

When it was winter, and the snow lay all around, white and sparkling, a hare would often come jumping along, and spring right over the little Fir Tree. Oh! this made him so angry. But two winters went by, and when the third came the little Tree had grown so tall that the hare was obliged to run round it.

"Oh! to grow, to grow, and become old; that's the only fine thing in the world," thought the Tree.

In the autumn woodcutters always came and felled a few of the largest trees; that was done this year too, and the little Fir Tree, that was now quite well grown, shuddered with fear, for the great stately trees fell to the ground with a crash, and their branches were cut off, so that the trees looked quite naked, long, and slender—they could hardly be recognized. But then they were laid upon waggons, and horses dragged them away out of the wood. Where were they going? What destiny awaited them?

In the spring, when the swallows and the Stork came, the Tree asked them, "Do you know where they were taken? Did you not meet them?"

The swallows knew nothing about it, but the Stork looked thoughtful, nodded his head, and said,

"Yes, I think so. I met many new ships when I flew out of Egypt; on the ships were stately masts; I fancy that these were the trees. They smelt like fir. I can assure you they're stately—very stately."

"Oh that I were only big enough to go over the sea! What kind of thing is this sea, and how does it look?"

"It would take too long to explain all that," said the Stork, and he went away.

"Rejoice in thy youth," said the Sunbeams; "rejoice in thy fresh growth, and in the young life that is within thee."

And the wind kissed the Tree, and the dew wept tears upon it; but the Fir Tree did not understand that.

When Christmas-time approached, quite young trees were felled, sometimes trees which were neither so old nor so large as this Fir Tree, that never rested but always wanted to go away. These young trees, which were almost the most beautiful, kept all their branches; they were put upon waggons, and horses dragged them away out of the wood.

"Where are they all going?" asked the Fir Tree. "They are not greater than I—indeed, one of them was much smaller. Why do they keep all their branches? Whither are they taken?"

"We know that! We know that!" chirped the Sparrows. "Yonder in the town we looked in at the windows. We know where they go. Oh! they are dressed up in the greatest pomp and splendour that can be imagined. We have looked in at the windows, and have perceived that they are planted in the middle of the warm room, and adorned with the most beautiful things—gilt apples, honey-cakes, playthings, and many hundreds of candles."

"And then?" asked the Fir Tree, and trembled through all its branches. "And then? What happens then?"

"Why, we have not seen anything more. But it was incomparable."

"Perhaps I may be destined to tread this glorious path one day!" cried the Fir Tree rejoicingly. "That is even better than travelling across the sea. How painfully I long for it! If it were only Christmas now! Now I am great and grown up, like the rest who were led away last year. Oh, if I were only on the carriage! If I were only in the warm room, among all the pomp and splendour! And then? Yes, then something even better will come, something far more charming, or else why should they adorn me so? There must be something grander, something greater still to come; but what? Oh! I'm suffering, I'm longing! I don't know myself what is the matter with me!"

"Rejoice in us," said Air and Sunshine. "Rejoice in thy fresh youth here in the woodland."

But the Fir Tree did not rejoice at all, but it grew and grew; winter and summer it stood there, green, dark green. The people who saw it said, "That's a handsome tree!" and at Christmas-time it was felled before any one of the others. The axe cut deep into its marrow, and the tree fell to the ground with a sigh: it felt a pain, a sensation of faintness, and could not think at all of happiness, for it was sad at parting from its home, from the place where it had grown up: it knew that it should never again see the dear old companions, the little bushes and flowers all around—perhaps not even the birds. The parting was not at all agreeable.

The Tree only came to itself when it was unloaded in a yard, with other trees, and heard a man say,

"This one is famous; we only want this one!"

Now two servants came in gay liveries, and carried the Fir Tree into a large beautiful saloon. All around the walls hung pictures, and by the great stove stood large Chinese vases with lions on the covers; there were rocking-chairs, silken sofas, great tables covered with picture-books, and toys worth a hundred times a hundred dollars, at least the children said so. And the Fir Tree was put into a great tub filled with sand; but no one could see that it was a tub, for it was hung round with green cloth, and stood on a large many-coloured carpet. Oh, how the Tree trembled! What was to happen now? The servants, and the young ladies also, decked it out. On one branch they hung little nets, cut out of coloured paper; every net was filled with sweetmeats; golden apples and walnuts hung down as if they grew there, and more than a hundred little candles, red, white, and blue, were fastened to the different boughs. Dolls that looked exactly like real people—the Tree had never seen such before—swung among the foliage, and high on the summit of the Tree was fixed a tinsel star. It was splendid, particularly splendid.

"This evening," said all, "this evening it will shine."

"Oh," thought the Tree, "that it were evening already! Oh that the lights may be soon lit up! When may that be done? I wonder if trees will come out of the forest to look at me? Will the sparrows fly against the panes? Shall I grow fast here, and stand adorned in summer and winter?"

Yes, he did not guess badly. But he had a complete backache from mere longing, and the backache is just as bad for a Tree as the headache for a person.

At last the candles were lighted. What a brilliance, what splendour! The Tree trembled so in all its branches that one of the candles set fire to a green twig, and it was scorched.

"Heaven preserve us!" cried the young ladies; and they hastily put the fire out.

Now the Tree might not even tremble. Oh, that was terrible! It was so afraid of setting fire to some of its ornaments, and it was quite bewildered with all the brilliance. And now the folding doors were thrown open, and a number of children rushed in as if they would have overturned the whole Tree; the older people followed more deliberately. The little ones stood quite silent, but only for a minute; then they shouted till the room rang: they danced gleefully round the Tree, and one present after another was plucked from it.

"What are they about?" thought the Tree. "What's going to be done?"

And the candles burned down to the twigs, and as they burned down they were extinguished, and then the children received permission to plunder the Tree. Oh! they rushed in upon it, so that every branch cracked again: if it had not been fastened by the top and by the golden star to the ceiling, it would have fallen down.

The children danced about with their pretty toys. No one looked at the Tree except one old man, who came up and peeped among the branches, but only to see if a fig or an apple had not been forgotten.

"A story! a story!" shouted the children: and they drew a little fat man towards the Tree; and he sat down just beneath it,—"for then we shall be in the green wood," said he, "and the tree may have the advantage of listening to my tale. But I can only tell one. Will you hear the story of Ivede-Avede, or of Klumpey-Dumpey, who fell down stairs, and still was raised up to honour and married the Princess?"

"Ivede-Avede!" cried some, "Klumpey-Dumpey!" cried others, and there was a great crying and shouting. Only the Fir Tree was quite silent, and thought, "Shall I not be in it? shall I have nothing to do in it?" but he had been in the evening's amusement, and had done what was required of him.

And the fat man told about Klumpey-Dumpey, who fell down stairs, and yet was raised to honour and married the Princess. And the children clapped their hands, and cried, "Tell another! tell another!" for they wanted to hear about Ivede-Avede; but they only got the story of Klumpey-Dumpey. The Fir Tree stood quite silent and thoughtful; never had the birds in the wood told such a story as that.

Klumpey-Dumpey fell down stairs, and yet came to honour and married the Princess!

"Yes, so it happens in the world!" thought the Fir Tree, and believed it must be true, because that was such a nice man who told it. "Well, who can know? Perhaps I shall fall down stairs too, and marry a Princess!" And it looked forward with pleasure to being adorned again, the next evening, with candles and toys, gold and fruit. "To-morrow I shall not tremble," it thought. "I will rejoice in all my splendour. To-morrow I shall hear the story of Klumpey-Dumpey again, and, perhaps, that of Ivede-Avede too."

And the Tree stood all night quiet and thoughtful.

In the morning the servants and the chambermaid came in.

"Now my splendour will begin afresh," thought the Tree. But they dragged him out of the room, and up stairs to the garret, and here they put him in a dark corner where no daylight shone.

"What's the meaning of this?" thought the Tree. "What am I to do here? What is to happen?"

And he leaned against the wall, and thought, and thought. And he had time enough, for days and nights went by, and nobody came up; and when at length some one came, it was only to put some great boxes in a corner. Now the Tree stood quite hidden away, and the supposition was that it was quite forgotten.

"Now it's winter outside," thought the Tree. "The earth is hard and covered with snow, and people cannot plant me; therefore I suppose I'm to be sheltered here until spring comes. How considerate that is! How good people are! If it were only not so dark here, and so terribly solitary!—not even a little hare! That was pretty out there in the wood, when the snow lay thick and the hare sprang past; yes, even when he jumped over me; but then I did not like it. It is terribly lonely up here!"

"Piep! piep!" said a little Mouse, and crept forward, and then came another little one. They smelt at the Fir Tree, and then slipped among the branches.

"It's horribly cold," said the two little Mice, "or else it would be comfortable here. Don't you think so, you old Fir Tree?"

"I'm not old at all," said the Fir Tree. "There are many much older than I."

"Where do you come from?" asked the Mice. "And what do you know?" They were dreadfully inquisitive. "Tell us about the most beautiful spot on earth. Have you been there? Have you been in the store-room, where cheeses lie on the shelves, and hams hang from the ceiling, where one dances on tallow candles, and goes in thin and comes out fat?"

"I don't know that!" replied the Tree; "but I know the wood, where the sun shines, and where the birds sing."

And then it told all about its youth.

And the little Mice had never heard anything of the kind; and they listened and said,

"What a number of things you have seen! How happy you must have been!"

"I?" said the Fir Tree; and it thought about what it had told. "Yes, those were really quite happy times." But then he told of the Christmas-eve, when he had been hung with sweetmeats and candles.

"Oh!" said the little Mice, "how happy you have been, you old Fir Tree!"

"I'm not old at all," said the Tree. "I only came out of the wood this winter. I'm only rather backward in my growth."

"What splendid stories you can tell!" said the little Mice.

And next night they came with four other little Mice, to hear what the Tree had to relate; and the more it said, the more clearly did it remember everything, and thought, "Those were quite merry days! But they may come again. Klumpey-Dumpey fell down stairs, and yet he married the Princess. Perhaps I may marry a Princess too!" And then the Fir Tree thought of a pretty little birch tree that grew out in the forest: for the Fir Tree, that birch was a real Princess.

"Who's Klumpey-Dumpey?" asked the little Mice.

And then the Fir Tree told the whole story. It could remember every single word; and the little Mice were ready to leap to the very top of the tree with pleasure. Next night a great many more Mice came, and on Sunday two Rats even appeared; but these thought the story was not pretty, and the little Mice were sorry for that, for now they also did not like it so much as before.

"Do you only know one story?" asked the Rats.

"Only that one," replied the Tree. "I heard that on the happiest evening of my life; I did not think then how happy I was."

"That's a very miserable story. Don't you know any about bacon and tallow candles—a store-room story?"

"No," said the Tree.

"Then we'd rather not hear you," said the Rats.

And they went back to their own people. The little Mice at last stayed away also; and then the Tree sighed and sighed and said,

"It was very nice when they sat round me, the merry little Mice, and listened when I spoke to them. Now that's past too. But I shall remember to be pleased when they take me out."

But when did that happen? Why, it was one morning that people came and rummaged in the garret: the boxes were put away, and the Tree brought out; they certainly threw him rather roughly on the floor, but a servant dragged him away at once to the stairs, where the daylight shone.

"Now life is beginning again!" thought the Tree.

It felt the fresh air and the first sunbeams, and now it was out in the courtyard. Everything passed so quickly that the Tree quite forgot to look at itself, there was so much to look at all round. The courtyard was close to a garden, and here everything was blooming; the roses hung fresh and fragrant over the little paling, the linden trees were in blossom, and the swallows cried, "Quinze-wit! quinze-wit! my husband's come!" But it was not the Fir Tree that they meant.

"Now I shall live!" said the Tree, rejoicingly, and spread its branches far out; but, alas! they were all withered and yellow; and it lay in the corner among nettles and weeds. The tinsel star was still upon it, and shone in the bright sunshine.

In the courtyard a couple of the merry children were playing, who had danced round the tree at Christmas-time, and had rejoiced over it. One of the youngest ran up and tore off the golden star.

"Look what is sticking to the ugly old fir tree," said the child, and he trod upon the branches till they cracked again under his boots.

And the Tree looked at all the blooming flowers and the splendour of the garden, and then looked at itself, and wished it had remained in the dark corner of the garret; it thought of its fresh youth in the wood, of the merry Christmas-eve, and of the little Mice which had listened so pleasantly to the story of Klumpey-Dumpey.

"Past! past!" said the old Tree. "Had I but rejoiced when I could have done so! Past! past!"

And the servant came and chopped the Tree into little pieces; a whole bundle lay there. It blazed brightly under the great brewing copper, and it sighed deeply, and each sigh was like a little shot; and the children who were at play there ran up and seated themselves at the fire, looked into it, and cried, "Puff! puff!" But at each explosion, which was a deep sigh, the tree thought of a summer day in the woods, or of a winter night there, when the stars beamed; he thought of Christmas-eve and of Klumpey-Dumpey, the only story he had ever heard or knew how to tell; and then the Tree was burned.

The boys played in the garden, and the youngest had on his breast a golden star, which the Tree had worn on its happiest evening. Now that was past, and the Tree's life was past, and the story is past too: past! past!—and that's the way with all stories.

The Goblins and the Sexton

—from *The Pickwick Papers*

by CHARLES DICKENS

IN an old abbey town, down in this part of the country, a long, long while ago—so long, that the story must be a true one, because our great-grandfathers implicitly believed it—there officiated as sexton and grave-digger in the churchyard, one Gabriel Grub. It by no means follows that because a man is a sexton, and constantly surrounded by the emblems of mortality, therefore he should be a morose and melancholy man; your undertakers are the merriest fellows in the world; and I once had the honour of being on intimate terms with a mute, who in private life, and off duty, was as comical and jocose a little fellow as ever chirped out a devil-may-care song, without a hitch in his memory, or drained off the contents of a good stiff glass without stopping for breath. But, notwithstanding these precedents to the contrary, Gabriel Grub was an ill-conditioned, cross-grained, surly fellow—a morose and lonely man, who consorted with nobody but himself, and an old wicker bottle which fitted into his large deep waistcoat pocket—and who eyed each merry face, as it passed him by, with such a deep scowl of malice and ill-humour, as it was difficult to meet, without feeling something the worse for.

A little before twilight, one Christmas eve, Gabriel shouldered his spade, lighted his lantern, and betook himself towards the old churchyard; for he had got a grave to finish by next morning, and, feeling very low, he thought it might raise his spirits, perhaps, if he went on with his work at once. As he went his way, up the ancient street, he saw the cheerful light of the blazing fires gleam through the old casements, and heard the loud laugh and the cheerful shouts of those who were assembled around them; he marked the bustling preparations for next day's cheer, and smelt the numerous savoury odours consequent thereupon, as they steamed up from the kitchen windows in clouds. All this was gall and wormwood to the heart of Gabriel Grub; and when groups of children bounded out of the houses, tripped across the road, and were met, before they could knock at the opposite door, by half a dozen curly-headed little rascals who crowded round them as they flocked upstairs to spend the evening in their Christmas games, Gabriel smiled grimly, and clutched the handle of his spade with a firmer grasp, as he thought of measles, scarlet-fever, thrush, whooping-cough, and a good many other sources of consolation besides.

In this happy frame of mind, Gabriel strode along: returning a short, sullen growl to the good-humoured greetings of such of his neighbours as now and then passed him: until he turned into the dark lane which led to the churchyard. Now, Gabriel had been looking forward to reaching the dark lane, because it was, generally speaking, a nice, gloomy, mournful place, into which the towns-people did not much care to go, except in broad daylight, and when the sun was shining; consequently, he was not a little indignant to hear a young urchin roaring out some jolly song about a merry Christmas, in this very sanctuary, which had been called Coffin Lane ever since the days of the old abbey, and the time of the shaven-headed monks. As Gabriel walked on, and the voice drew nearer, he found it proceeded from a small boy, who was hurrying along, to join one of the little parties in the old street, and who, partly to keep himself company, and partly to prepare himself for the occasion, was shouting out the song at the highest pitch of his lungs. So Gabriel waited until the boy came up, and then dodged him into a corner, and rapped him over the head with his lantern five or six times, to teach him to modulate his voice. And as the boy hurried away with his hand to his head, singing quite a different sort of tune, Gabriel Grub chuckled very heartily to himself, and entered the churchyard: locking the gate behind him.

He took off his coat, put down his lantern, and getting into the unfinished grave, worked at it for an hour or so, with right good will. But the earth was hardened with the frost, and it was no very easy matter to break it up, and shovel it out; and although there was a moon, it was a very young one, and shed little light upon the grave, which was in the shadow of the church. At any other time, these obstacles would have made Gabriel Grub very moody and miserable, but he was so well pleased with having stopped the small boy's singing, that he took little heed of the scanty progress he had made, and looked down into the grave, when he had finished work for the night, with grim satisfaction, murmuring as he gathered up his things:

"Brave lodgings for one, brave lodgings for one,
A few feet of cold earth, when life is done;
A stone at the head, a stone at the feet,
A rich, juicy meal for the worms to eat;
Rank grass overhead, and damp clay around,
Brave lodgings for one, these, in holy ground!

"Ho! ho!" laughed Gabriel Grub, as he sat himself down on a flat tombstone which was a favourite resting-place of his; and drew forth his wicker bottle. "A coffin at Christmas! A Christmas Box. Ho! ho! ho!"

"Ho! ho! ho!" repeated a voice which sounded close behind him.

Gabriel paused, in some alarm, in the act of raising the wicker bottle to his lips; and looked round. The bottom of the oldest grave about him, was not more still and quiet, than the churchyard in the pale moonlight. The cold hoar-frost glistened on the tombstones, and sparkled like rows of gems, among the stone carvings of the old church. The snow lay hard and crisp upon the ground; and spread over the thickly-strewn mounds of earth so white and smooth a cover that it seemed as if corpses lay there, hidden only by their winding sheets. Not the faintest rustle broke the profound tranquillity of the solemn scene. Sound itself appeared to be frozen up, all was so cold and still.

"It was the echoes," said Gabriel Grub, raising the bottle to his lips again.

"It was *not*," said a deep voice.

Gabriel started up, and stood rooted to the spot with astonishment and terror; for his eyes rested on a form that made his blood run cold.

Seated on an upright tombstone, close to him, was a strange unearthly figure, whom Gabriel felt at once, was no being of this world. His long fantastic legs which might have reached the ground, were cocked up, and crossed after a quaint, fantastic fashion; his sinewy arms were bare; and his hands rested on his knees. On his short round body, he wore a close covering, ornamented with small slashes; a short cloak dangled at his back; the collar was cut into curious peaks, which served the goblin in lieu of ruff or neckerchief; and his shoes curled up at his toes into long points. On his head, he wore a broad-brimmed sugar-loaf hat, garnished with a single feather. The hat was covered with the white frost; and the goblin looked as if he had sat on the same tombstone very comfortably, for two or three hundred years. He was sitting perfectly still; his tongue was put out, as if in derision; and he was grinning at Gabriel Grub with such a grin as only a goblin could call up.

"It was *not* the echoes," said the goblin.

Gabriel Grub was paralysed, and could make no reply.

"What do you do here on Christmas eve?" said the goblin sternly.

"I came to dig a grave, sir," stammered Gabriel Grub.

"What man wanders among graves and churchyards on such a night as this?" cried the goblin.

"Gabriel Grub! Gabriel Grub!" screamed a wild chorus of voices that seemed to fill the churchyard. Gabriel looked fearfully round—nothing was to be seen.

"What have you got in that bottle?" said the goblin.

"Hollands, sir," replied the sexton, trembling more than ever; for he had bought it of the smugglers, and he thought that perhaps his questioner might be in the excise department of the goblins.

"Who drinks Hollands alone, and in a churchyard, on such a night as this?" said the goblin.

"Gabriel Grub! Gabriel Grub!" exclaimed the wild voices again.

The goblin leered maliciously at the terrified sexton, and then raising his voice, exclaimed:

"And who, then, is our fair and lawful prize?"

To this inquiry the invisible chorus replied, in a strain that sounded like the voices of many choristers singing to the mighty swell of the old church organ—a strain that seemed borne to the sexton's ears upon a wild wind, and to die away as it passed onward; but the burden of the reply was still the same, "Gabriel Grub! Gabriel Grub!"

The goblin grinned a broader grin than before, as he said, "Well, Gabriel, what do you say to this?"

The sexton gasped for breath.

"What do you think of this, Gabriel?" said the goblin, kicking up his feet in the air on either side of the tombstone, and looking at the turned-up points with as much complacency as if he had been contemplating the most fashionable pair of Wellingtons in all Bond Street.

"It's—it's—very curious, sir," replied the sexton, half dead with fright; "very curious, and very pretty, but I think I'll go back and finish my work, sir, if you please."

"Work!" said the goblin, "what work?"

"The grave, sir; making the grave," stammered the sexton.

"Oh, the grave, eh?" said the goblin; "who makes graves at a time when all other men are merry, and takes a pleasure in it?"

Again the mysterious voices replied, "Gabriel Grub! Gabriel Grub!"

"I'm afraid my friends want you, Gabriel," said the goblin, thrusting his tongue further into his cheek than ever—and a most astonishing tongue it was. "I'm afraid my friends want you, Gabriel," said the goblin.

"Under favour, sir," replied the horror-stricken sexton, "I don't think they can, sir; they don't know me, sir; I don't think the gentlemen have ever seen me, sir."

"Oh yes they have," replied the goblin; "we know the man with the sulky face and grim scowl, that came down the street to-night, throwing his evil looks at the children, and grasping his burying spade the tighter. We know the man who struck the boy in the envious malice of his heart, because the boy could be merry, and he could not. We know him, we know him."

Here, the goblin gave a loud shrill laugh, which the echoes returned twenty-fold: and throwing his legs up in the air, stood upon his head, or rather upon the very point of his sugar-loaf hat, on the narrow edge of the tombstone: whence he threw a somerset with extraordinary agility, right to the sexton's feet, at which he planted himself in the attitude in which tailors generally sit upon the shop-board.

"I—I—am afraid I must leave you, sir," said the sexton, making an effort to move.

"Leave us!" said the goblin, "Gabriel Grub going to leave us. Ho! ho! ho!"

As the goblin laughed, the sexton observed, for one instant, a brilliant illumination within the windows of the church, as if the whole building were lighted up; it disappeared, the organ pealed forth a lively air, and whole troops of goblins, the very counterpart of the first one, poured into the churchyard, and began playing at leap-frog with the tombstones: never stopping for an instant to take breath, but 'overing' the highest among them, one after the other, with the most marvellous dexterity. The first goblin was a most astonishing leaper, and none of the others could come near him; even in the extremity of his terror the sexton could not help observing, that while his friends were content to leap over the common-sized gravestones, the first one took the family vaults, iron railings and all, with as much ease as if they had been so many street posts.

At last the game reached to a most exciting pitch; the organ played quicker and quicker; and the goblins leaped faster and faster: coiling themselves up, rolling head over heels upon the ground, and bounding over the tombstones like foot-balls. The sexton's brain whirled round with the rapidity of the motion he beheld, and his legs reeled beneath him, as the spirits flew before his eyes: when the goblin king, suddenly darting towards him, laid his hand upon his collar, and sank with him through the earth.

When Gabriel Grub had had time to fetch his breath, which the rapidity of his descent had for the moment taken away, he found himself in what appeared to be a large cavern, surrounded on all sides by crowds of goblins, ugly and grim; in the centre of the room, on an elevated seat, was stationed his friend of the churchyard; and close beside him stood Gabriel Grub himself, without power of motion.

"Cold to-night," said the king of the goblins, "very cold. A glass of something warm, here!"

At this command, half a dozen officious goblins, with a perpetual smile upon their faces, whom Gabriel Grub imagined to be courtiers, on that account, hastily disappeared, and presently returned with a goblet of liquid fire, which they presented to the king.

"Ah!" cried the goblin, whose cheeks and throat were transparent, as he tossed down the flame, "This warms one, indeed! Bring a bumper of the same, for Mr. Grub."

It was in vain for the unfortunate sexton to protest that he was not in the habit of taking anything warm at night; one of the goblins held him while another poured the blazing liquid down his throat; the whole assembly screeched with laughter as he coughed and choked, and wiped away the tears which gushed plentifully from his eyes, after swallowing the burning draught.

"And now," said the king, fantastically poking the taper corner of his sugar-loaf hat into the sexton's eye, and thereby occasioning him the most exquisite pain: "And now, show the man of misery and gloom, a few of the pictures from our own great storehouse!"

As the goblin said this, a thick cloud which obscured the remoter end of the cavern, rolled gradually away, and disclosed, apparently at a great distance, a small and scantily furnished, but neat and clean apartment. A crowd of little children were gathered round a bright fire, clinging to their mother's gown, and gambolling around her chair. The mother occasionally rose, and drew aside the window-curtain, as if to look for some expected object: a frugal meal was ready spread upon the table; and an elbow chair was placed near the fire. A knock was heard at the door: the mother opened it, and the children crowded round her, and clapped their hands for joy, as their father entered. He was wet and weary, and shook the snow from his garments, as the children crowded round him, and seizing his cloak, hat, stick, and gloves, with busy zeal, ran with them from the room. Then, as he sat down to his meal before the fire, the children climbed about his knee, and the mother sat by his side, and all seemed happiness and comfort.

But a change came upon the view, almost imperceptibly. The scene was altered to a small bed-room, where the fairest and youngest child lay dying; the roses had fled from his cheek, and the light from the eye; and even as the sexton looked upon him with an interest he had never felt or known before, he died. His young brothers and sisters crowded round his little bed, and seized his tiny hand, so cold and heavy; but they shrunk back from its touch, and looked with awe on his infant face; for calm and tranquil as it was and sleeping in rest and peace as the beautiful child seemed to be, they saw that he was dead, and they knew that he was an Angel looking down upon, and blessing them, from a bright and happy Heaven.

Again the light cloud passed across the picture, and again the subject changed. The father and mother were old and helpless now, and the number of those about them was diminished more than half; but content and cheerfulness sat on every face, and beamed in every eye, as they crowded round the fireside, and told and listened to old stories of earlier and bygone days. Slowly and peacefully, the father sank into the grave, and, soon after, the sharer of all his cares and troubles followed him to a place of rest. The few, who yet survived them, knelt by their tomb, and watered the green turf which covered it, with their tears; then rose, and turned away: sadly and mournfully, but not with bitter cries, or despairing lamentations, for they knew that they should one day meet again; and once more they mixed with the busy world, and their content and cheerfulness were restored. The cloud settled upon the picture, and concealed it from the sexton's view.

"What do you think of *that*?" said the goblin, turning his large face toward Gabriel Grub.

Gabriel murmured out something about its being very pretty, and looked somewhat ashamed, as the goblin bent his fiery eyes upon him.

"*You* a miserable man!" said the goblin, in a tone of excessive contempt. "You!" He appeared disposed to add more, but indignation choked his utterance, so he lifted up one of his very pliable legs, and flourishing it above his head a little, to insure his aim, administered a good sound kick to Gabriel Grub; immediately after which, all the goblins in waiting, crowded round the wretched sexton, and kicked him without mercy: according to the established and invariable custom of courtiers upon earth, who kick whom royalty kicks, and hug whom royalty hugs.

"Show him some more!" said the king of the goblins.

At these words, the cloud was dispelled, and a rich and beautiful landscape was disclosed to view—there is just such another, to this day, within half a mile of the old abbey town. The sun shone from out the clear blue sky, the water sparkled beneath his rays, and the trees looked greener, and the flowers more gay, beneath his cheering influence. The water rippled on, with a pleasant sound; the trees rustled in the light wind that murmured among their leaves; the birds sang upon the boughs; and the lark carolled on high her welcome to the morning. Yes, it was morning; the bright, balmy morning of summer; the minutest leaf, the smallest blade of grass, was instinct with life. The ant crept forth to her daily toil, the butterfly fluttered and basked in the warm rays of the sun; myriads of insects spread their transparent wings, and revelled in their brief but happy existence. Man walked forth, elated with the scene; and all was brightness and splendour.

"*You* a miserable man!" said the king of the goblins, in a more contemptuous tone than before. And again the king of the goblins gave his leg a flourish; again it descended on the shoulders of the sexton; and again the attendant goblins imitated the example of their chief.

Many a time the cloud went and came, and many a lesson it taught to Gabriel Grub, who, although his shoulders smarted with pain from the frequent applications of the goblins' feet, looked on with an interest that nothing could diminish. He saw that men who worked hard, and earned their scanty bread with lives of labour, were cheerful and happy; and that to the most ignorant, the sweet face of nature was a never-failing source of cheerfulness and joy. He saw those who had been delicately nurtured, and tenderly brought up, cheerful under privations, and superior to suffering that would have crushed many of a rougher grain, because they bore within their own bosoms the materials of happiness, contentment, and peace. He saw that women, the tenderest and most fragile of all God's creatures, were the oftenest superior to sorrow, adversity, and distress; and he saw that it was because they bore, in their own hearts, an inexhaustible well-spring of affection and devotion. Above all, he saw that men like himself, who snarled at the mirth and cheerfulness of others, were the foulest weeds on the fair surface of the earth; and setting all the good of the world against the evil, he came to the conclusion that it was a very decent and respectable sort of world after all. No sooner had he formed it, than the cloud which closed over the last picture, seemed to settle on his senses, and lull him to repose. One by one, the goblins faded from his sight; and as the last one disappeared, he sunk to sleep.

The day had broken when Gabriel Grub awoke, and found himself lying, at full length on the flat gravestone in the churchyard, with the wicker bottle lying empty by his side, and his coat, spade, and lantern, all well whitened by the last night's frost, scattered on the ground. The stone on which he had first seen the goblin seated, stood bolt upright before him, and the grave at which he had worked, the night before, was not far off. At first, he began to doubt the reality of his adventures, but the acute pain in his shoulders when he attempted to rise, assured him that the kicking of the goblins was certainly not ideal. He was staggered again by observing no traces of footsteps in the snow on which the goblins had played at leap-frog with the gravestones, but he speedily accounted for this circumstance when he remembered that, being spirits, they would leave no visible impression behind them. So, Gabriel Grub got on his feet as well as he could, for the pain in his back; and brushing the frost off his coat, put it on, and turned his face towards the town.

But he was an altered man, and he could not bear the thought of returning to a place where his repentance would be scoffed at, and his reformation disbelieved. He hesitated for a few moments; and then turned away to wander where he might, and seek his bread elsewhere.

The lantern, the spade, and the wicker bottle, were found, that day, in the churchyard. There were a great many speculations about the sexton's fate, at first, but it was speedily determined that he had been carried away by the goblins; and there were not wanting some very credible witnesses who had distinctly seen him whisked through the air on the back of a chestnut horse blind of one eye, with the hind-quarters of a lion, and the tail of a bear. At length all this was devoutly believed; and the new sexton used to exhibit to the curious, for a trifling emolument, a good-sized piece of the church weather-cock which had been accidentally kicked off by the aforesaid horse in his aerial flight, and picked up by himself in the churchyard, a year or two afterwards.

Unfortunately, these stories were somewhat disturbed by the unlooked-for reappearance of Gabriel Grub himself, some ten years afterwards, a ragged, contented, rheumatic old man. He told his story to the clergyman, and also to the mayor; and in course of time it began to be received, as a matter of history, in which form it has continued down to this very day. The believers in the weathercock tale, having misplaced their confidence once, were not easily prevailed upon to part with it again, so they looked as wise as they could, shrugged their shoulders, touched their foreheads, and murmured something about Gabriel Grub having drunk all the Hollands, and then fallen asleep on the flat tombstone; and they affected to explain what he supposed he had witnessed in the goblin's cavern, by saying that he had seen the world, and grown wiser. But this opinion, which was by no means a popular one at any time, gradually died off; and be the matter how it may, as Gabriel Grub was afflicted with rheumatism to the end of his days, this story has at least one moral, if it teach no better one—and that is, that if a man turn sulky and drink by himself at Christmas time, he may make up his mind to be not a bit the better for it: let the spirits be never so good, or let them be even as many degrees beyond proof, as those which Gabriel Grub saw in the goblin's cavern.

The Other Wise Man

by HENRY VAN DYKE

YOU know the story of the Three Wise Men of the East, and how they traveled from far away to offer their gifts at the manger cradle in Bethlehem. But have you ever heard the story of the Other Wise Man, who also saw the star in its rising, and set out to follow it, yet did not arrive with his brethren in the presence of the young child Jesus? Of the great desire of this fourth pilgrim, and how it was denied, yet accomplished in the denial; of his many wanderings and the probations of his soul; of the long way of his seeking and the strange way of his finding the One whom he sought—I would tell the tale as I have heard fragments of it in the Hall of Dreams, in the palace of the Heart of Man.

I

In the days when Augustus Caesar was master of many kings and Herod reigned in Jerusalem, there lived in the city of Ecbatana, among the mountains of Persia, a certain man named Artaban. His house stood close to the outermost of the walls which encircled the royal treasury. From his roof he could look over the sevenfold battlements of black and white and crimson and blue and red and silver and gold, to the hill where the summer palace of the Parthian emperors glittered like a jewel in a crown.

Around the dwelling of Artaban spread a fair garden, a tangle of flowers and fruit trees, watered by a score of streams descending from the slopes of Mount Orontes, and made musical by innumerable birds. But all color was lost in the soft and odorous darkness of the late September night, and all sounds were hushed in the deep charm of its silence, save the plashing of the water, like a voice half sobbing and half laughing under the shadows. High above the trees a dim glow of light shone through the curtained arches of the upper chamber, where the master of the house was holding council with his friends.

He stood by the doorway to greet his guests—a tall, dark man of about forty years, with brilliant eyes set near together under his broad brow, and firm lines graven around his fine, thin lips; the brow of a dreamer and the mouth of a soldier, a man of sensitive feeling but inflexible will—one of those who, in whatever age they may live, are born for inward conflict and a life of quest.

His robe was of pure white wool, thrown over a tunic of silk; and a white, pointed cap, with long lapels at the sides, rested on his flowing black hair. It was the dress of the ancient priesthood of the Magi, called the fire worshipers.

"Welcome!" he said, in his low, pleasant voice, as one after another entered the room—"welcome, Abdus; peace be with you, Rhodaspes and Tigranes, and with you, my father, Abgarus. You are all welcome. This house grows bright with the joy of your presence."

There were nine of the men, differing widely in age, but alike in the richness of their dress of many-colored silks, and in the massive golden collars around their necks, marking them as Parthian nobles, and in the winged circles of gold resting upon their breasts, the sign of the followers of Zoroaster.

They took their places around a small black altar at the end of the room, where a tiny flame was burning. Artaban, standing beside it, and waving a barsom of thin tamarisk branches above the fire, fed it with dry sticks of pine and fragrant oils. Then he began the ancient chant of the yasna, and the voices of his companions joined in the hymn to Ahura-Mazda:

We worship the Spirit Divine,
all wisdom and goodness possessing,
Surrounded by Holy Immortals,
the givers of bounty and blessing;
We joy in the work of His hands,
His truth and His power confessing.

We praise all the things that are pure,
for these are His only Creation;
The thoughts that are true and the words
and the deeds that have won approbation;
These are supported by Him,
and for these we make adoration.

Hear us, O Mazda! Thou livest
in truth and in heavenly gladness;
Cleanse us from falsehood, and keep us
from evil and bondage to badness;
Pour out the light and the joy of Thy life
on our darkness and sadness.

Shine on our gardens and fields,
shine on our working and weaving;
Shine on the whole race of man,
believing and unbelieving;

Shine on us now through the night,
Shine on us now in Thy might,
The flame of our holy love
and the song of our worship receiving.

The fire rose with the chant, throbbing as if the flame responded to the music, until it cast a bright illumination through the whole apartment, revealing its simplicity and splendor.

The floor was laid with tiles of dark blue veined with white; pilasters of twisted silver stood out against the blue walls; the clerestory of round-arched windows above them was hung with azure silk; the vaulted ceiling was a pavement of blue stones, like the body of heaven in its clearness, sown with silver stars. From the four corners of the roof hung four golden magic wheels, called the tongues of the gods. At the eastern end, behind the altar, there were two dark-red pillars of porphyry; above them a lintel of the same stone, on which was carved the figure of a winged archer, with his arrow set to the string and his bow drawn.

The doorway between the pillars, which opened upon the terrace of the roof, was covered with a heavy curtain of the color of a ripe pomegranate, embroidered with innumerable golden rays shooting upward from the floor. In effect the room was like a quiet, starry night, all azure and silver, flushed in the east with rosy promise of the dawn. It was, as the house of a man should be, an expression of the character and spirit of the master.

He turned to his friends when the song was ended, and invited them to be seated on the divan at the western end of the room.

"You have come tonight," said he, looking around the circle, "at my call, as the faithful scholars of Zoroaster, to renew your worship and rekindle your faith in the God of Purity, even as this fire has been rekindled on the altar. We worship not the fire, but Him of whom it is the chosen symbol, because it is the purest of all created things. It speaks to us of one who is Light and Truth. Is it not so, my father?"

"It is well said, my son," answered the venerable Abgarus. "The enlightened are never idolaters. They lift the veil of form and go in to the shrine of reality, and new light and truth are coming to them continually through the old symbols."

"Hear me, then, my father and my friends," said Artaban, "while I tell you of the new light and truth that have come to me through the most ancient of all signs. We have searched the secrets of Nature together, and studied the healing virtues of water and fire and the plants. We have read also the books of prophecy in which the future is dimly foretold in words that are hard to understand. But the highest of all learning is the knowledge of the stars. To trace their course is to untangle the threads of the mystery of life from the beginning to the end. If we could follow them perfectly, nothing would be hidden from us. But is not our knowledge of them still incomplete? Are there not many stars still beyond our horizon—lights that are known only to the dwellers in the far southland, among the spice trees of Punt and the gold mines of Ophir?"

There was a murmur of assent among the listeners.

"The stars," said Tigranes, "are the thoughts of the Eternal. They are numberless. But the thoughts of man can be counted, like the years of his life. The wisdom of the Magi is the greatest of all wisdoms on earth, because it knows its own ignorance. And that is the secret of power. We keep men always looking and waiting for a new sunrise. But we ourselves understand that the darkness is equal to the light, and that the conflict between them will never be ended."

"That does not satisfy me," answered Artaban, "for, if the waiting must be endless, if there could be no fulfillment of it, then it would not be wisdom to look and wait. We should become like those new teachers of the Greeks, who say that there is no truth, and that the only wise men are those who spend their lives in discovering and exposing the lies that have been believed in the world. But the new sunrise will certainly appear in the appointed time. Do not our own books tell us that this will come to pass, and that men will see the brightness of a great light?"

"That is true," said the voice of Abgarus; "every faithful disciple of Zoroaster knows the prophecy of the Avesta, and carries the word in his heart. 'In that day Sosiosh the Victorious shall arise out of the number of the prophets in the east country. Around him shall shine a mighty brightness, and he shall make life everlasting, incorruptible, and immortal, and the dead shall rise again.'"

"This is a dark saying," said Tigranes, "and it may be that we shall never understand it. It is better to consider the things that are near at hand, and to increase the influence of the Magi in their own country, rather than to look for one who may be a stranger, and to whom we must resign our power."

The others seemed to approve these words. There was a silent feeling of agreement manifest among them; their looks responded with that indefinable expression which always follows when a speaker has uttered the thought that has been slumbering in the hearts of his listeners. But Artaban turned to Abgarus with a glow on his face, and said:

"My father, I have kept this prophecy in the secret place of my soul. Religion without a great hope would be like an altar without a living fire. And now the flame has burned more brightly, and by the light of it I have read other words which also have come from the fountain of Truth, and speak yet more clearly of the rising of the Victorious One in his brightness."

He drew from the breast of his tunic two small rolls of fine parchment, with writing upon them, and unfolded them carefully upon his knee.

"In the years that are lost in the past, long before our fathers came into the land of Babylon, there were wise men in Chaldea, from whom the first of the Magi learned the secret of the heavens. And of these Balaam the son of Beor was one of the mightiest. Hear the words of his prophecy: 'There shall come a star out of Jacob, and a scepter shall arise out of Israel.'"

The lips of Tigranes drew downward with contempt, as he said:

"Judah was a captive by the waters of Babylon, and the sons of Jacob were in bondage to our kings. The tribes of Israel are scattered through the mountains like lost sheep, and from the remnant that dwells in Judea under the yoke of Rome neither star nor scepter shall arise."

"And yet," answered Artaban, "it was the Hebrew Daniel, the mighty searcher of dreams, the counselor of kings, the wise Belteshazzar, who was most honored and beloved of our great King Cyrus. A prophet of sure things and a reader of the thoughts of the Eternal, Daniel proved himself to our people. And these are the words that he wrote." (Artaban read from the second roll:) "'Know, therefore, and understand that from the going forth of the commandment to restore Jerusalem, unto the Anointed One, the Prince, the time shall be seven and threescore and two weeks.'"

"But, my son," said Abgarus, doubtfully, "these are mystical numbers. Who can interpret them, or who can find the key that shall unlock their meaning?"

Artaban answered: "It has been shown to me and to my three companions among the Magi—Caspar, Melchior and Balthasar. We have searched the ancient tablets of Chaldea and computed the time. It falls in this year. We have studied the sky, and in the spring of the year we saw two of the greatest planets draw near together in the sign of the Fish, which is the house of the Hebrews. We also saw a new star there, which shone for one night and then vanished. Now again the two great planets are meeting. This night is their conjunction. My three brothers are watching by the ancient Temple of the Seven Spheres, at Borsippa, in Babylonia, and I am watching here. If the star shines again, they will wait ten days for me at the temple, and then we will set out together for Jerusalem, to see and worship the promised one who shall be born King of Israel. I believe the sign will come. I have made ready for the journey. I have sold my possessions, and bought these three jewels—a sapphire, a ruby and a pearl—to carry them as tribute to the King. And I ask you to go with me on the pilgrimage, that we may have joy together in finding the Prince who is worthy to be served."

While he was speaking he thrust his hand into the inmost fold of his girdle and drew out three great gems—one blue as a fragment of the night sky, one redder than a ray of sunrise, and one as pure as the peak of a snow mountain at twilight—and laid them on the outspread scrolls before him.

But his friends looked on with strange and alien eyes. A veil of doubt and mistrust came over their faces, like a fog creeping up from the marshes to hide the hills. They glanced at each other with looks of wonder and pity, as those who have listened to incredible sayings, the story of a wild vision, or the proposal of an impossible enterprise.

At last Tigranes said: "Artaban, this is a vain dream. It comes from too much looking upon the stars and the cherishing of lofty thoughts. It would be wiser to spend the time in gathering money for the new fire temple at Chala. No king will ever rise from the broken race of Israel, and no end will ever come to the eternal strife of light and darkness. He who looks for it is a chaser of shadows. Farewell."

And another said: "Artaban, I have no knowledge of these things, and my office as guardian of the royal treasure binds me here. The quest is not for me. But if thou must follow it, fare thee well."

And another said: "In my house there sleeps a new bride, and I cannot leave her nor take her with me on this strange journey. This quest is not for me. But may thy steps be prospered wherever thou goest. So, farewell."

And another said: "I am ill and unfit for hardship, but there is a man among my servants whom I will send with thee when though goest, to bring me word how thou farest."

So, one by one, they left the house of Artaban. But Abgarus, the oldest and the one who loved him the best, lingered after the others had gone, and said, gravely: "My son, it may be that the light of truth is in this sign that has appeared in the skies, and then it will surely lead to the Prince and the mighty brightness. Or it may be that it is only a shadow of the light, as Tigranes has said, and then he who follows it will have a long pilgrimage and fruitless search. But it is better to follow even the shadow of the best than to remain content with the worst. And those who would see wonderful things must often be ready to travel alone. I am too old for this journey, but my heart shall be a companion of thy pilgrimage day and night, and I shall know the end of thy quest. Go in peace."

Then Abgarus went out of the azure chamber with its silver stars, and Artaban was left in solitude.

He gathered up the jewels and replaced them in his girdle. For a long time he stood and watched the flame that flickered and sank upon the altar. Then he crossed the hall, lifted the heavy curtain, and passed out between the pillars of porphyry to the terrace on the roof.

The shiver that runs through the earth ere she rouses from her night sleep had already begun, and the cool wind that heralds the daybreak was drawing downward from the lofty, snow-traced ravines of Mount Orontes. Birds, half-awakened, crept and chirped among the rustling leaves, and the smell of ripened grapes came in brief wafts from the arbors.

Far over the eastern plain a white mist stretched like a lake. But where the distant peaks of Zagros serrated the western horizon the sky was clear. Jupiter and Saturn rolled together like drops of lambent flame about to blend in one.

As Artaban watched them, a steel-blue spark was born out of the darkness beneath, rounding itself with purple splendors to a crimson sphere, and spiring upward through rays of saffron and orange into a point of white radiance. Tiny and infinitely remote, yet perfect in every part, it pulsated in the enormous vault as if the three jewels in the

Magian's girdle had mingled and been transformed into a living heart of light.

He bowed his head. He covered his brow with his hands.

"It is the sign," he said. "The King is coming, and I will go to meet him."

II

All night long, Vasda, the swiftest of Artaban's horses, had been waiting, saddled and bridled, in her stall, pawing the ground impatiently and shaking her bit as if she shared the eagerness of her master's purpose, though she knew not its meaning.

Before the birds had fully roused to their strong, high, joyful chant of morning song, before the white mist had begun to lift lazily from the plain, the Other Wise Man was in the saddle, riding swiftly along the highroad, which skirted the base of Mount Orontes, westward.

How close, how intimate is the comradeship between a man and his favourite horse on a long journey. It is a silent, comprehensive friendship, an intercourse beyond the need of words.

They drink at the same wayside springs, and sleep under the same guardian stars. They are conscious together of the subduing spell of nightfall and the quickening joy of daybreak. The master shares his evening meal with his hungry companion, and feels the soft, moist lips caressing the palm of his hand as they close over the morsel of bread. In the gray dawn he is roused from his bivouac by the gentle stir of a warm, sweet breath over his sleeping face, and looks up into the eyes of his faithful fellow traveler, ready and waiting for the toil of the day. Surely, unless he is a pagan and an unbeliever, by whatever name he calls upon his God, he will thank Him for this voiceless sympathy, this dumb affection, and his morning prayer will embrace a double blessing—God bless us both, the horse and the rider, and keep our feet from falling and our souls from death!

Then, through the keen morning air, the swift hoofs beat their tattoo along the road, keeping time to the pulsing of two hearts that are moved with the same eager desire—to conquer space, to devour the distance, to attain the goal of the journey.

Artaban must indeed ride wisely and well if he would keep the appointed hour with the other Magi; for the route was a hundred and fifty parasangs, and fifteen was the utmost that he could travel in a day. But he knew Vasda's strength, and pushed forward without anxiety, making the fixed distance every day, though he must travel late into the night, and in the morning long before sunrise.

He passed along the brown slopes of Mount Orontes, furrowed by the rocky courses of a hundred torrents.

He crossed the level plains of the Nicaeans, where the famous herds of horses, feeding in the wide pastures, tossed their heads at Vasda's approach, and galloped away with a thunder of many hoofs, and flocks of wild birds rose suddenly from the swampy meadows, wheeling in great circles with a shining flutter of innumerable wings and shrill cries of surprise.

He traversed the fertile fields of Concabar, where the dust from the threshing floors filled the air with a golden mist, half hiding the huge temple of Astarte with its four hundred pillars.

At Baghistan, among the rich gardens watered by fountains from the rock, he looked up at the mountain thrusting its immense rugged brow out over the road, and saw the figure of King Darius trampling upon his fallen foes, and the proud list of his wars and conquests graven high upon the face of the eternal cliff.

Over many a cold and desolate pass, crawling painfully across the wind-swept shoulders of the hills; down many a black mountain gorge, where the river roared and raced before him like a savage guide; across many a smiling vale, with terraces of yellow limestone full of vines and fruit trees; through the oak groves of Carine and the dark Gates of Zagros, walled in by precipices; into the ancient city of Chala, where the people of Samaria had been kept in captivity long ago; and out again by the mighty portal, riven through the encircling hills, where he saw the image of the High Priest of the Magi sculptured on the wall of rock, with hand uplifted as if to bless the centuries of pilgrims; past the entrance of the narrow defile, filled from end to end with orchards of peaches and figs, through which the river Gyndes foamed down to meet him; over the broad rich fields, where the autumnal vapors spread their deathly mists; following along the course of the river, under tremulous shadows of poplar and tamarind, among the lower hills; and out upon the flat plain, where the road ran straight as an arrow through the stubble fields and parched meadows; past the city of Ctesiphon, where the Parthian emperors reigned, and the vast metropolis of Seleucia which Alexander built; across the swirling floods of Tigris and the many channels of Euphrates, flowing yellow through the cornlands—Artaban pressed onward until he arrived, at nightfall on the tenth day, beneath the shattered walls of populous Babylon.

Vasda was almost spent, and Artaban would gladly have turned into the city to find rest and refreshment for himself and for her. But he knew that it was three hours' journey yet to the Temple of the Seven Spheres, and he must reach the place by midnight if he would find his comrades waiting. So he did not halt, but rode steadily across the stubble fields.

A grove of date palms made an island of gloom in the pale yellow sea. As she passed into the shadow Vasda slackened her pace, and began to pick her way more carefully.

Near the farther end of the darkness an access of caution seemed to fall upon her. She scented some danger or difficulty; it was not in her heart to fly from it—only to be prepared for it, and to meet it wisely, as a good horse should do. The grove was close and silent as the tomb; not a leaf rustled, not a bird sang.

She felt her steps before her delicately, carrying her head low, and sighing now and then with apprehension. At last she gave a quick breath of anxiety and dismay, and stood stock-still, quivering in every muscle, before a dark object in the shadow of the last palm tree.

Artaban dismounted. The dim starlight revealed the form of a man lying across the road. His humble dress and the outline of his haggard face showed that he was probably one of the Hebrews who still dwelt in great numbers around the city. His pallid skin, dry and yellow as parchment, bore the mark of the deadly fever which ravaged the marshlands in autumn. The chill of death was in his lean hand, and, as Artaban released it, the arm fell back inertly upon the motionless breast.

He turned away with a thought of pity, leaving the body to that strange burial which the Magians deemed most fitting—the funeral of the desert, from which the kites and vultures rise on dark wings, and the beasts of prey slink furtively away. When they are gone there is only a heap of white bones on the sand.

But, as he turned, a long, faint, ghostly sigh came from the man's lips. The bony fingers gripped the hem of the Magian's robe and held him fast.

Artaban's heart leaped to his throat, not with fear, but with a dumb resentment at the importunity of this blind delay.

How could he stay here in the darkness to minister to a dying stranger? What claim had this unknown fragment of human life upon his compassion or his service? If he lingered but for an hour he could hardly reach Borsippa at the appointed time. His companions would think he had given up the journey. They would go without him. He would lose his quest.

But if he went on now, the man would surely die. If Artaban stayed, life might be restored. His spirit throbbed and fluttered with the urgency of the crisis. Should he risk the great reward of his faith for the sake of a single deed of charity? Should he turn aside, if only for a moment, from the following of the star, to give a cup of cold water to a poor, perishing Hebrew?

"God of truth and purity," he prayed, "direct me in the holy path, the way of wisdom which Thou only knowest."

Then he turned back to the sick man. Loosening the grasp of his hand, he carried him to a little mound at the foot of the palm tree.

He unbound the thick folds of the turban and opened the garment above the sunken breast. He brought water from one of the small canals near by, and moistened the sufferer's brow and mouth. He mingled a draught of one of those simple but potent remedies which he carried always in his girdle—for the Magians were physicians as well as astrologers—and poured it slowly between the colorless lips. Hour after hour he labored as only a skillful healer of disease can do. At last the man's strength returned; he sat up and looked about him.

"Who art thou?" he said, in the rude dialect of the country, "and why hast thou sought me here to bring back my life?"

"I am Artaban the Magian, of the city of Ecbatana, and I am going to Jerusalem in search of one who is to be born King of the Jews, a great Prince and Deliverer of all men. I dare not delay any longer upon my journey, for the caravan that has waited for me may depart without me. But see, here is all that I have left of bread and wine, and here is a potion of healing herbs. When thy strength is restored thou canst find the dwellings of the Hebrews among the houses of Babylon."

The Jew raised his trembling hand solemnly to heaven.

"Now may the God of Abraham and Isaac and Jacob bless and prosper the journey of the merciful, and bring him in peace to his desired haven. Stay! I have nothing to give thee in return—only this: that I can tell thee where the Messiah must be sought. For our prophets have said that he should be born not in Jerusalem, but in Bethlehem of Judah. May the Lord bring thee in safety to that place, because thou hast had pity upon the sick."

It was already long past midnight. Artaban rode in haste, and Vasda, restored by the brief rest, ran eagerly through the silent plain and swam the channels of the river. She put forth the remnant of her strength and fled over the ground like a gazelle.

But the first beam of the rising sun sent a long shadow before her as she entered upon the final stadium of the journey, and the eyes of Artaban, anxiously scanning the great mound of Nimrod and the Temple of the Seven Spheres, could discern no trace of his friends.

The many-colored terraces of black and orange and red and yellow and green and blue and white, shattered by the convulsions of nature, and crumbling under the repeated blows of human violence, still glittered like a ruined rainbow in the morning light.

Artaban rode swiftly around the hill. He dismounted and climbed to the highest terrace, looking out toward the west. The huge desolation of the marshes stretched away to the horizon and the border of the desert. Bitterns stood by the stagnant pools and jackals skulked through the low bushes; but there was no sign of the caravan of the Wise Men, far or near.

At the edge of the terrace he saw a little cairn of broken bricks, and under them a piece of papyrus. He caught it up and read: "We have waited past the midnight, and can delay no longer. We go to find the King. Follow us across the desert."

Artaban sat down upon the ground and covered his head in despair.

"How can I cross the desert," said he, "with no food and with a spent horse? I must return to Babylon, sell my sapphire, and buy a train of camels, and provision for the journey. I may never overtake my friends. Only God the merciful knows whether I shall not lose the sight of the King because I tarried to show mercy."

III

There was a silence in the Hall of Dreams, where I was listening to the story of the Other Wise Man. Through this silence I saw, but very dimly, his figure passing over the dreary undulations of the desert, high upon the back of his camel, rocking steadily onward like a ship over the waves.

The land of death spread its cruel net around him. The stony waste bore no fruit but briers and thorns. The dark ledges of rock thrust themselves above the surface here and there, like the bones of perished monsters. Arid and inhospitable mountain ranges rose before him, furrowed with dry channels of ancient torrents, white and ghastly as scars on the face of nature. Shifting hills of treacherous sand were heaped like tombs along the horizon. By day the fierce heat pressed its intolerable burden on the quivering air. No living creature moved on the dumb, swooning earth, but tiny jerboas scuttling through the parched bushes, or lizards vanishing in the clefts of the rock. By night the jackals prowled and barked in the distance, and the lion made the black ravines echo with his hollow roaring, while a bitter, blighting chill followed the fever of the day. Through heat and cold, the Magian moved steadily onward.

Then I saw the gardens and orchards of Damascus, watered by the streams of Abana and Pharpar, with their sloping swards inlaid with bloom, and their thickets of myrrh and roses. I saw the long, snowy ridge of Hermon, and the dark groves of cedars, and the valley of the Jordan, and the blue waters of the Lake of Galilee, and the fertile plain of Esdraelon, and the hills of Ephraim, and the highlands of

Judah. Through all these I followed the figure of Artaban moving steadily onward, until he arrived at Bethlehem. And it was the third day after the three Wise Men had come to that place and had found Mary and Joseph, with the young child, Jesus, and had laid their gifts of gold and frankincense and myrrh at his feet.

Then the Other Wise Man drew near, weary, but full of hope, bearing his ruby and his pearl to offer to the King. "For now at last," he said, "I shall surely find him, though I be alone, and later than my brethren. This is the place of which the Hebrew exile told me that the prophets had spoken, and here I shall behold the rising of the great light. But I must inquire about the visit of my brethren, and to what house the star directed them, and to whom they presented their tribute."

The streets of the village seemed to be deserted, and Artaban wondered whether the men had all gone up to the hill pastures to bring down their sheep. From the open door of a cottage he heard the sound of a woman's voice singing softly. He entered and found a young mother hushing her baby to rest. She told him of the strangers from the far East who had appeared in the village three days ago, and how they said that a star had guided them to the place where Joseph of Nazareth was lodging with his wife and her new-born child, and how they had paid reverence to the child and given him many rich gifts.

"But the travelers disappeared again," she continued, "as suddenly as they had come. We were afraid at the strangeness of their visit. We could not understand it. The man of Nazareth took the child and his mother, and fled away that same night secretly, and it was whispered that they were going to Egypt. Ever since, there has been a spell upon the village; something evil hangs over it. They say that the Roman soldiers are coming from Jerusalem to force a new tax from us, and the men have driven the flocks and herds far back among the hills, and hidden themselves to escape it."

Artaban listened to her gentle, timid speech, and the child in her arms looked up in his face and smiled, stretching out its rosy hands to grasp at the winged circle of gold on his breast. His heart warmed to the touch. It seemed like a greeting of love and trust to one who had journeyed long in loneliness and perplexity, fighting with his own doubts and fears, and following a light that was veiled in clouds.

"Why might not this child have been the promised Prince?" he asked within himself, as he touched its soft cheek. "Kings have been born ere now in lowlier houses than this, and the favorite of the stars may rise even from a cottage. But it has not seemed good to the God of wisdom to reward my search so soon and so easily. The one whom I seek has gone before me; and now I must follow the King to Egypt."

The young mother laid the baby in its cradle, and rose to minister to the wants of the strange guest that fate had brought into her house. She set food before him, the plain fare of peasants, but willingly offered, and therefore full of refreshment for the soul as well as for the body. Artaban accepted it gratefully; and, as he ate, the child fell into a happy slumber, and murmured sweetly in its dreams, and a great peace filled the room.

But suddenly there came the noise of a wild confusion in the streets of the village, a shrieking and wailing of women's voices, a clangor of brazen trumpets and a clashing of swords, and a desperate cry: "The soldiers! The soldiers of Herod! They are killing our children."

The young mother's face grew white with terror. She clasped her child to her bosom, and crouched motionless in the darkest corner of the room, covering him with the folds of her robe, lest he should wake and cry.

But Artaban went quickly and stood in the doorway of the house. His broad shoulders filled the portal from side to side, and the peak of his white cap all but touched the lintel.

The soldiers came hurrying down the street with bloody hands and dripping swords. At the sight of the stranger in his imposing dress they hesitated with surprise. The captain of the band approached the threshold to thrust him aside. But Artaban did not stir. His face was as calm as though he were watching the stars, and in his eyes there burned that steady radiance before which even the half-tamed hunting leopard shrinks, and the bloodhound pauses in his leap. He held the soldier silently for an instant, and then said in a low voice:

"I am all alone in this place, and I am waiting to give this jewel to the prudent captain who will leave me in peace."

He showed the ruby, glistening in the hollow of his hand like a great drop of blood.

The captain was amazed at the splendor of the gem. The pupils of his eyes expanded with desire, and the hard lines of greed wrinkled around his lips. He stretched out his hand and took the ruby.

"March on!" he cried to his men; "there is no child here. The house is empty."

The clamor and the clang of arms passed down the street as the headlong fury of the chase sweeps by the secret covert where the trembling deer is hidden. Artaban re-entered the cottage. He turned his face to the east and prayed:

"God of truth, forgive my sin! I have said the thing that is not, to save the life of a child. And two of my gifts are gone. I have spent for man that which was meant for God. Shall I ever be worthy to see the face of the King?"

But the voice of the woman, weeping for joy in the shadow behind him, said very gently:

"Because thou hast saved the life of my little one, may the Lord bless thee and keep thee; the Lord make His face to shine upon thee and be gracious unto thee; the Lord lift up His countenance upon thee and give thee peace."

IV

Again there was a silence in the Hall of Dreams, deeper and more mysterious than the first interval, and I understood that the years of Artaban were flowing very swiftly under the stillness, and I caught only a glimpse, here and there, of the river of his life shining through the mist that concealed its course.

I saw him moving among the throngs of men in populous Egypt, seeking everywhere for traces of the household that had come down from Bethlehem, and finding them under the spreading sycamore trees of Heliopolis, and beneath the walls of the Roman fortress of New Babylon beside the Nile—traces so faint and dim that they vanished before him continually, as footprints on the wet river sand glisten for a moment with moisture and then disappear.

I saw him again at the foot of the pyramids, which lifted their sharp points into the intense saffron glow of the sunset sky, changeless monuments of the perishable glory and the imperishable hope of man. He looked up into the face of the crouching Sphinx and vainly tried to read the meaning of the calm eyes and smiling mouth. Was it, indeed, the mockery of all effort and all aspiration, as Tigranes had said—the cruel jest of a riddle that has no answer, a search that never can succeed? Or was there a touch of pity and encouragement in that inscrutable smile—a promise that even the defeated should attain victory, and the disappointed should discover a prize, and the ignorant should be made wise, and the blind should see, and the wandering should come into the haven at last?

I saw him again in an obscure house of Alexandria, taking counsel with a Hebrew rabbi. The venerable man, bending over the rolls of parchment on which the prophecies of Israel were written, read aloud the pathetic words which foretold the sufferings of the promised Messiah—the despised and rejected of men, the man of sorrows and acquainted with grief.

"And remember, my son," said he, fixing his eyes upon the face of Artaban, "the King whom thou seekest is not to be found in a palace, nor among the rich and powerful. If the light of the world and the glory of Israel had been appointed to come with the greatness of earthly splendor, it must have appeared long ago. For no son of Abraham will ever again rival the power which Joseph had in the palaces of Egypt, or the magnificence of Solomon throned between the lions in Jerusalem. But the light for which the world is waiting is a new light, the glory that shall rise out of patient and triumphant suffering. And the kingdom which is to be established forever is a new kingdom, the royalty of unconquerable love.

"I do not know how this shall come to pass, nor how the turbulent kings and peoples of earth shall be brought to acknowledge the Messiah and pay homage to him. But this I know. Those who seek him will do well to look among the poor and the lowly, the sorrowful and the oppressed."

So I saw the Other Wise Man again and again, traveling from place to place, and searching among the people of the Dispersion, with whom the little family from Bethlehem might, perhaps, have found a refuge. He passed through countries where famine lay heavy upon the land, and the poor were crying for bread. He made his dwelling in plague-stricken cities where the sick were languishing in the bitter companionship of helpless misery. He visited the oppressed and the afflicted in the gloom of subterranean prisons, and the crowded wretchedness of slave markets, and the weary toil of galley ships. In all this populous and intricate world of anguish, though he found none to worship, he found many to help. He fed the hungry, and clothed the naked, and healed the sick, and comforted the captive; and his years passed more swiftly than the weaver's shuttle that flashes back and forth through the loom while the web grows and the pattern is completed.

It seemed almost as if he had forgotten his quest. But once I saw him for a moment as he stood alone at sunrise, waiting at the gate of a Roman prison. He had taken from a secret resting place in his bosom the pearl, the last of his jewels. As he looked at it, a mellower luster, a soft and iridescent light, full of shifting gleams of azure and rose, trembled upon its surface. It seemed to have absorbed some reflection of the lost sapphire and ruby. So the secret purpose of a noble life draws into itself the memories of past joy and past sorrow. All that has helped it, all that has hindered it, is tranfused by a subtle magic into its very essence. It becomes more luminous and precious the longer it is carried close to the warmth of the beating heart.

Then, at last, while I was thinking of this pearl, and of its meaning, I heard the end of the story of the Other Wise Man.

V

Three-and-thirty years of the life of Artaban had passed away, and he was still a pilgrim and a seeker after light. His hair, once darker than the cliffs of Zagros, was now white as the wintry snow that covered them. His eyes, that once flashed like flames of fire, were dull as embers smoldering among the ashes.

Worn and weary and ready to die, but still looking for the King, he had come for the last time to Jerusalem. He had often visited the Holy City before, and had searched all its lanes and crowded hovels and black prisons without finding any trace of the family of Nazarenes who had fled from Bethlehem long ago. But now it seemed as if he must make one more effort, and something whispered in his heart that, at last, he might succeed.

It was the season of the Passover. The city was thronged with strangers. The children of Israel, scattered in far lands, had returned to the Temple for the great feast, and there had been a confusion of tongues in the narrow streets for many days.

But on this day a singular agitation was visible in the multitude. The sky was veiled with a portentous gloom. Currents of excitement seemed to flash through the crowd. A secret tide was sweeping them all one way. The clatter of sandals and the soft, thick sound of thousands of bare feet shuffling over the stones, flowed unceasingly along the street that leads to the Damascus gate.

Artaban joined a group of people from his own country, Parthian Jews who had come up to keep the Passover, and inquired of them the cause of the tumult, and where they were going.

"We are going," they answered, "to the place called Golgatha, outside the city walls, where there is to be an execution. Have you not heard what has happened? Two famous robbers are to be crucified, and with them another, called Jesus of Nazareth, a man who has done many wonderful works among the people, so that they love him greatly. But the priests and elders have said that he must die, because he gave himself out to be the Son of God. And Pilate has sent him to the cross because he said that he was the 'King of the Jews.'"

How strangely these familiar words fell upon the tired heart of Artaban! They had led him for a lifetime over land and sea. And now they came to him mysteriously, like a message of despair. The King had arisen, but he had been denied and cast out. He was about to perish. Perhaps he was already dying. Could it be the same who had been born in Bethlehem thirty-three years ago, at whose birth the star had appeared in heaven, and of whose coming the prophets had spoken?

Artaban's heart beat unsteadily with that troubled, doubtful apprehension which is the excitement of old age. But he said within himself: "The ways of God are stranger than the thoughts of men, and it may be that I shall find the King, at last, in the hands of his enemies, and shall come in time to offer my pearl for his ransom before he dies."

So the old man followed the multitude with slow and painful steps toward the Damascus gate of the city. Just beyond the entrance of the guardhouse a troop of Macedonian soldiers came down the street, dragging a young girl with torn dress and disheveled hair. As the Magian paused to look at her with compassion, she broke suddenly from the hands of the tormentors, and threw herself at his feet, clasping him around the knees. She had seen his white cap and the winged circle on his breast.

"Have pity on me," she cried, "and save me, for the sake of the God of Purity! I also am a daughter of the true religion which is taught by the Magi. My father was a merchant of Parthia, but he is dead, and I am seized for his debts to be sold as a slave. Save me from worse than death!"

Artaban trembled.

It was the old conflict in his soul, which had come to him in the palm grove of Babylon and in the cottage at Bethlehem—the conflict between the expectation of faith and the impulse of love. Twice the gift which he had consecrated to the worship of religion had been drawn to the service of humanity. This was the third trial, the ultimate probation, the final and irrevocable choice.

Was it his great opportunity, or his last temptation? He could not tell. One thing only was clear in the darkness of his mind—it was inevitable. And does not the inevitable come from God?

One thing only was sure to his divided heart—to rescue this helpless girl would be a true deed of love. And is not love the light of the soul?

He took the pearl from his bosom. Never had it seemed so luminous, so radiant, so full of tender, living luster. He laid it in the hand of the slave.

"This is thy ransom, daughter! It is the last of my treasures which I kept for the King."

While he spoke, the darkness of the sky deepened, and shuddering tremors ran through the earth heaving convulsively like the breast of one who struggles with mighty grief.

The walls of the houses rocked to and fro. Stones were loosened and crashed into the street. Dust clouds filled the air. The soldiers fled in terror, reeling like drunken men. But Artaban and the girl whom he had ransomed crouched helpless beneath the wall of the Praetorium.

What had he to fear? What had he to hope? He had given away the last remnant of his tribute for the King. He had parted with the last hope of finding him. The quest was over, and it had failed. But even in that thought, accepted and embraced, there was peace. It was not resignation. It was not submission. It was something more profound and searching. He knew that all was well, because he had done the best that he could from day to day. He had been true to the light that had been given to him. He had looked for more. And if he had not found it, if a failure was all that came out of his life, doubtless that was the best that was possible. He had not seen the revelation of "life everlasting, incorruptible and immortal." But he knew that even if he could live his earthly life over again, it could not be otherwise than it had been.

One more lingering pulsation of the earthquake quivered through the ground. A heavy tile, shaken from the roof, fell and struck the old man on the temple. He lay breathless and pale, with his gray head resting on the young girl's shoulder, and the blood trickling from the wound. As she bent over him, fearing that he was dead, there came a voice through the twilight, very small and still, like music sounding from a distance, in which the notes are clear but the words are lost. The girl turned to see if someone had spoken from the window above them, but she saw no one.

Then the old wise man's lips began to move, as if in answer, and she heard him say in the Parthian tongue:

"Not so, my Lord! For when saw I thee hungered and fed thee? Or thirsty, and gave thee drink? When saw I thee a stranger, and took thee in? Or naked, and clothed thee? When saw I thee sick or in prison, and came unto thee? Three-and-thirty years have I looked for thee; but I have never seen thy face, nor ministered to thee, my King."

He ceased, and the sweet voice came again. And again the maid heard it, very faint and far away. But now it seemed as though she understood the words:

"Verily I say unto thee, Inasmuch as thou has done it unto one of the least of these my brethren, thou hast done it unto me."

A calm radiance of wonder and joy lighted the pale face of Artaban like the first ray of dawn on a snowy mountain peak. A long breath of relief exhaled gently from his lips.

His journey was ended. His treasures were accepted. The Other Wise Man had found the King.

The Holy Night

by SELMA LAGERLÖF

THERE was a man who went out in the dark night to borrow live coals to kindle a fire. He went from hut to hut and knocked. "Dear friends, help me!" said he. "My wife has just given birth to a child, and I must make a fire to warm her and the little one."

But it was way in the night, and all the people were asleep. No one replied.

The man walked and walked. At last he saw the gleam of a fire a long way off. Then he went in that direction, and saw that the fire was burning in the open. A lot of sheep were sleeping around the fire, and an old shepherd sat and watched over the flock.

When the man who wanted to borrow fire came up to the sheep, he saw that three big dogs lay asleep at the shepherd's feet. All three awoke when the man approached and opened their great jaws, as though they wanted to bark; but not a sound was heard. The man noticed that the hair on their backs stood up and that their sharp, white teeth glistened in the firelight. They dashed toward him. He felt that one of them bit at his leg and one at his hand and that one clung to his throat. But their jaws and teeth wouldn't obey them, and the man didn't suffer the least harm.

Now the man wished to go farther, to get what he needed. But the sheep lay back to back and so close to one another that he couldn't pass them. Then the man stepped upon their backs and walked over them and up to the fire. And not one of the animals awoke or moved.

When the man had almost reached the fire, the shepherd looked up. He was a surly old man, who was unfriendly and harsh toward human beings. And when he saw the strange man coming, he seized the long piked staff, which he always held in his hand when he tended his flock, and threw it at him. The staff came right toward the man, but, before it reached him, it turned off to one side and whizzed past him, far out in the meadow.

Now the man came up to the shepherd and said to him: "Good man, help me, and lend me a little fire! My wife has just given birth to a child, and I must make a fire to warm her and the little one."

The shepherd would rather have said no, but when he pondered that the dogs couldn't hurt the man, and the sheep had not run from him, and that the staff had not wished to strike him, he was a little afraid, and dared not deny the man that which he asked.

"Take as much as you need!" he said to the man.

But then the fire was nearly burnt out. There were no logs or branches left, only a big heap of live coals; and the stranger had neither spade nor shovel, wherein he could carry the red-hot coals.

When the shepherd saw this, he said again: "Take as much as you need!" And he was glad that the man wouldn't be able to take away any coals.

But the man stooped and picked coals from the ashes with his bare hands, and laid them in his mantle. And he didn't burn his hands when he touched them, nor did the coals scorch his mantle; but he carried them away as if they had been nuts or apples.

And when the shepherd, who was such a cruel and hard-hearted man, saw all this, he began to wonder to himself: "What kind of a night is this, when the dogs do not bite, the sheep are not scared, the staff does not kill, or the fire scorch?" He called the stranger back, and said to him: "What kind of a night is this? And how does it happen that all things show you compassion?"

Then said the man: "I cannot tell you if you yourself do not see it." And he wished to go his way, that he might soon make a fire and warm his wife and child.

But the shepherd did not wish to lose sight of the man before he had found out what all this might portend. He got up and followed the man till they came to the place where he lived.

Then the shepherd saw that the man didn't have so much as a hut to dwell in, but that his wife and babe were lying in a mountain grotto, where there was nothing except the cold and naked stone walls.

But the shepherd thought that perhaps the poor innocent child might freeze to death there in the grotto; and, although he was a hard man, he was touched, and thought he would like to help it. And he loosened his knapsack from his shoulder, took from it a soft white sheepskin, gave it to the strange man, and said that he should let the child sleep on it.

But just as soon as he showed that he, too, could be merciful, his eyes were opened, and he saw what he had not been able to see before and heard what he could not have heard before.

He saw that all around him stood a ring of little silver-winged angels, and each held a stringed instrument, and all sang in loud tones that tonight the Saviour was born who should redeem the world from its sins.

Then he understood how all things were so happy this night that they didn't want to do anything wrong.

And it was not only around the shepherd that there were angels, but he saw them everywhere. They sat inside the grotto, they sat outside on the mountain, and they flew under the heavens. They came marching in great companies, and, as they passed, they paused and cast a glance at the child.

There were such jubilation and such gladness and songs and play! And all this he saw in the dark night, whereas before he could not have made out anything. He was so happy because his eyes had been opened that he fell upon his knees and thanked God.

What that shepherd saw, we might also see, for the angels fly down from heaven every Christmas Eve, if we could only see them.

You must remember this, for it is as true, as true as that I see you and you see me. It is not revealed by the light of lamps or candles, and it does not depend upon sun and moon; but that which is needful is that we have such eyes as can see God's glory.

The Little Match Girl

by HANS CHRISTIAN ANDERSEN

IT was terribly cold; it snowed and was already almost dark, and evening came on, the last evening of the year. In the cold and gloom a poor little girl, bare-headed and barefoot, was walking through the streets. When she left her own house she certainly had had slippers on; but of what use were they? They were very big slippers, and her mother had used them till then, so big were they. The little maid lost them as she slipped across the road, where two carriages were rattling by terribly fast. One slipper was not to be found again, and a boy had seized the other, and run away with it. He thought he could use it very well as a cradle, some day when he had children of his own. So now the little girl went with her little naked feet, which were quite red and blue with the cold. In an old apron she carried a number of matches, and a bundle of them in her hand. No one had bought anything of her all day, and no one had given her a farthing.

Shivering with cold and hunger she crept along, a picture of misery, poor little girl! The snow-flakes covered her long fair hair, which fell in pretty curls over her neck; but she did not think of that now. In all the windows lights were shining, and there was a glorious smell of roast goose, for it was New Year's Eve. Yes, she thought of that!

In a corner formed by two houses, one of which projected beyond the other, she sat down, cowering. She had drawn up her little feet, but she was still colder, and she did not dare to go home, for she had sold no matches, and did not bring a farthing of money. From her father she would certainly receive a beating, and besides, it was cold at home, for they had nothing over them but a roof through which the wind whistled, though the largest rents had been stopped with straw and rags.

Her little hands were almost benumbed with the cold. Ah! a match might do her good, if she could only draw one from the bundle, and rub it against the wall, and warm her hands at it. She drew one out. R-r-atch!—how it sputtered and burned! It was a warm bright flame, like a little candle, when she held her hands over it; it was a wonderful little light! It really seemed to the little girl as if she sat before a great polished stove, with bright brass feet and a brass cover. How the fire burned! How comfortable it was! But the little flame went out, the stove vanished, and she had only the remains of the burned match in her hand.

A second was rubbed against the wall. It burned up, and when the light fell upon the wall it became transparent like a thin veil, and she could see through it into the room. On the table a snow-white cloth was spread; upon it stood a shining dinner service; the roast goose smoked gloriously, stuffed with apples and dried plums. And what was still more splendid to behold, the goose hopped down from the dish, and waddled along the floor, with a knife and fork in its breast, to the little girl. Then the match went out, and only the thick, damp, cold wall was before her. She lighted another match. Then she was sitting under a beautiful Christmas tree; it was greater and more ornamented than the one she had seen through the glass door at the rich merchant's. Thousands of candles burned upon the green branches, and coloured pictures like those in the print shops looked down upon them. The little girl stretched forth her hand towards them; then the match went out. The Christmas lights mounted higher. She saw them now as stars in the sky: one of them fell down, forming a long line of fire.

"Now some one is dying," thought the little girl, for her old grandmother, the only person who had loved her, and who was now dead, had told her that when a star fell down a soul mounted up to God.

She rubbed another match against the wall; it became bright again, and in the brightness the old grandmother stood clear and shining, mild and lovely.

"Grandmother!" cried the child, "Oh! take me with you! I know you will go when the match is burned out. You will vanish like the warm fire, the warm food, and the great glorious Christmas tree!"

And she hastily rubbed the whole bundle of matches, for she wished to hold her grandmother fast. And the matches burned with such a glow that it became brighter than in the middle of the day; grandmother had never been so large or so beautiful. She took the little girl in her arms, and both flew in brightness and joy above the earth, very, very high, and up there was neither cold, nor hunger, nor care—they were with God!

But in the corner, leaning against the wall, sat the poor girl with red cheeks and smiling mouth, frozen to death on the last evening of the Old Year. The New Year's sun rose upon a little corpse! The child sat there, stiff and cold, with the matches of which one bundle was burned. "She wanted to warm herself," the people said. No one imagined what a beautiful thing she had seen, and in what glory she had gone in with her grandmother to the New Year's Day.

The Gift of the Magi

by O. HENRY

ONE dollar and eighty-seven cents. That was all. And sixty cents of it was in pennies. Pennies saved one and two at a time by bulldozing the grocer and the vegetable man and the butcher until one's cheeks burned with the silent imputation of parsimony that such close dealing implied. Three times Della counted it. One dollar and eighty-seven cents. And the next day would be Christmas.

There was clearly nothing to do but flop down on the shabby little couch and howl. So Della did it. Which instigates the moral reflection that life is made up of sobs, sniffles, and smiles, with sniffles predominating.

While the mistress of the home is gradually subsiding from the first stage to the second, take a look at the home. A furnished flat at eight dollars per week. It did not exactly beggar description, but it certainly had that word on the lookout for the mendicancy squad.

In the vestibule below was a letter-box into which no letter would go, and an electric button from which no mortal finger could coax a ring. Also appertaining thereunto was a card bearing the name "Mr. James Dillingham Young."

The "Dillingham" had been flung to the breeze during a former period of prosperity when its possessor was being paid thirty dollars per week. Now, when the income was shrunk to twenty dollars, the letters of "Dillingham" looked blurred, as though they were thinking seriously of contracting to a modest and unassuming D. But whenever Mr. James Dillingham Young came home and reached his flat above he was called "Jim" and greatly hugged by Mrs. James Dillingham Young, already introduced to you as Della. Which is all very good.

Della finished her cry and attended to her cheeks with a powder-puff. She stood by the window and looked out dully at a gray cat walking a gray fence in a gray back yard. Tomorrow would be Christmas Day, and she had only $1.87 with which to buy Jim a present. She had been saving every penny she could for months, with this result. Twenty dollars a week doesn't go far. Expenses had been greater than she had calculated. They always are. Only $1.87 to buy a present for Jim. Her Jim. Many a happy hour she had spent planning for something nice for him. Something fine and rare and sterling—something just a little bit near to being worthy of the honor of being owned by Jim.

There was a pier-glass between the windows of the room. Perhaps you have seen a pier-glass in an eight-dollar flat. A very thin and very agile person may, by observing his reflection in a rapid sequence of longitudinal strips, obtain a fairly accurate conception of his looks. Della, being slender, had mastered the art.

Suddenly she whirled from the window and stood before the glass. Her eyes were shining brilliantly, but her face had lost its color within twenty seconds. Rapidly she pulled down her hair and let it fall to its full length.

Now, there were two possessions of the James Dillingham Youngs in which they both took a mighty pride. One was Jim's gold watch that had been his father's and his grandfather's. The other was Della's hair. Had the Queen of Sheba lived in the flat across the airshaft, Della would have let her hair hang out the window some day to dry just to depreciate Her Majesty's jewels and gifts. Had King Solomon been the janitor, with all his treasures piled up in the basement, Jim would have pulled out his watch every time he passed, just to see him pluck at his beard from envy.

So now Della's beautiful hair fell about her, rippling and shining like a cascade of brown waters. She did it up again nervously and quickly. Once she faltered for a minute and stood still while a tear or two splashed on the worn red carpet.

On went her old brown jacket; on went her old brown hat. With a whirl of skirts and with the brilliant sparkle still in her eyes, she fluttered out the door and down the stairs to the street.

Where she stopped the sign read: "Mme. Sofronie. Hair Goods of All Kinds." One flight up Della ran, and collected herself, panting. Madame, large, too white, chilly, hardly looked the "Sofronie."

"Will you buy my hair?" asked Della.

"I buy hair," said Madame. "Take yer hat off and let's have a sight at the looks of it."

Down rippled the brown cascade.

"Twenty dollars," said Madame, lifting the mass with a practiced hand.

"Give it to me quick," said Della.

Oh, and the next two hours tripped by on rosy wings. Forget the hashed metaphor. She was ransacking the stores for Jim's present.

She found it at last. It surely had been made for Jim and no one else. There was no other like it in any of the stores, and she had turned all of them inside out. It was a platinum watch-chain, simple and chaste in design, properly proclaiming its value by substance alone and not by meretricious ornamentation—as all good things should do. It was even worthy of The Watch. As soon as she saw it she knew that it must be Jim's. It was like him. Quietness and value—the description applied to both. Twenty-one dollars they took from her for it, and she hurried home with the eighty-seven cents. With that chain on his watch Jim might be properly anxious about the time in any company. Grand as the watch was, he sometimes looked at it on the sly on account of the old leather strap that he used in place of a chain.

When Della reached home her intoxication gave way a little to prudence and reason. She got out her curling-irons and lighted the gas and went to work repairing the ravages made by generosity added to love. Which is always a tremendous task, dear friends—a mammoth task.

Within forty minutes her head was covered with tiny close-lying curls that made her look wonderfully like a truant school-boy. She looked at her reflection in the mirror long, carefully, and critically.

"If Jim doesn't kill me," she said to herself, "before he takes a second look at me, he'll say I look like a Coney Island chorus girl. But what could I do—oh! what could I do with a dollar and eighty-seven cents?"

At seven o'clock the coffee was made and the frying-pan was on the back of the stove, hot and ready to cook the chops.

Jim was never late. Della doubled the watch-chain in her hand and sat on the corner of the table near the door that he always entered. Then she heard his step on the stair away down on the first flight, and she turned white for just a moment. She had a habit of saying little silent prayers about the simplest everyday things, and now she whispered: "Please, God, make him think I am still pretty."

The door opened and Jim stepped in and closed it. He looked thin and very serious. Poor fellow, he was only twenty-two—and to be burdened with a family! He needed a new overcoat and he was without gloves.

Jim stepped inside the door, as immovable as a setter at the scent of quail. His eyes were fixed upon Della, and there was an expression in them that she could not read, and it terrified her. It was not anger, nor surprise, nor disapproval, nor horror, nor any of the sentiments that she had been prepared for. He simply stared at her fixedly with that peculiar expression on his face.

Della wriggled off the table and went for him.

"Jim, darling," she cried, "don't look at me that way. I had my hair cut off and sold it because I couldn't have lived through Christmas without giving you a present. It'll grow out again—you won't mind, will you? I just had to do it. My hair grows awfully fast. Say 'Merry Christmas!' Jim, and let's be happy. You don't know what a nice—what a beautiful, nice gift I've got for you."

"You've cut off your hair?" asked Jim, laboriously, as if he had not arrived at that patent fact yet even after the hardest mental labor.

"Cut it off and sold it," said Della. "Don't you like me just as well, anyhow? I'm me without my hair, ain't I?"

Jim looked about the room curiously.

"You say your hair is gone?" he said, with an air almost of idiocy.

"You needn't look for it," said Della. "It's sold, I tell you—sold and gone, too. It's Christmas Eve, boy. Be good to me, for it went for you. Maybe the hairs of my head were numbered," she went on with a sudden serious sweetness, "but nobody could ever count my love for you. Shall I put the chops on, Jim?"

Out of his trance Jim seemed to quickly wake. He enfolded his Della. For ten seconds let us regard with discreet scrutiny some inconsequential object in the other direction. Eight dollars a week or a million a year—what is the difference? A mathematician or a wit would give you the wrong answer. The Magi brought valuable gifts, but that was not among them. This dark assertion will be illuminated later on.

Jim drew a package from his overcoat pocket and threw it upon the table.

"Don't make any mistake, Dell," he said, "about me. I don't think there's anything in the way of a haircut or a shave or a shampoo that could make me like my girl any less. But if you'll unwrap that package you may see why you had me going awhile at first."

White fingers and nimble tore at the string and paper. And then an ecstatic scream of joy; and then, alas! a quick feminine change to hysterical tears and wails, necessitating the immediate employment of all the comforting powers of the lord of the flat.

For there lay The Combs—the set of combs that Della had worshiped for long in a Broadway window. Beautiful combs, pure tortoise shell, with jeweled rims—just the shade to wear in the beautiful vanished hair. They were expensive combs, she knew, and her heart had simply craved and yearned over them without the least hope of possession. And now they were hers, but the tresses that should have adorned the coveted adornments were gone.

But she hugged them to her bosom, and at length she was able to look up with dim eyes and a smile and say: "My hair grows so fast, Jim!"

And then Della leaped up like a little singed cat and cried, "Oh, oh!"

Jim had not yet seen his beautiful present. She held it out to him eagerly upon her open palm. The dull precious metal seemed to flash with a reflection of her bright and ardent spirit.

"Isn't it a dandy, Jim? I hunted all over town to find it. You'll have to look at the time a hundred times a day now. Give me your watch. I want to see how it looks on it."

Instead of obeying, Jim tumbled down on the couch and put his hands under the back of his head and smiled.

"Dell," he said, "let's put our Christmas presents away and keep 'em awhile. They're too nice to use just at present. I sold the watch to get the money to buy your combs. And now suppose you put the chops on."

The Magi, as you know, were wise men—wonderfully wise men—who brought gifts to the Babe in the manger. They invented the art of giving Christmas presents. Being wise, their gifts were no doubt wise ones, possibly bearing the privilege of exchange in case of duplication. And here I have lamely related to you the uneventful chronicle of two foolish children in a flat who most unwisely sacrificed for each other the greatest treasures of their house. But in a last word to the wise of these days let it be said that of all who give gifts these two were the wisest. Of all who give and receive gifts, such as they are wisest. Everywhere they are wisest. They are the Magi.

The Cratchits' Christmas Dinner

—from *A Christmas Carol*

by CHARLES DICKENS

HIS active little crutch was heard upon the floor, and back came Tiny Tim before another word was spoken, escorted by his brother and sister to his stool before the fire; and while Bob, turning up his cuffs—as if, poor fellow, they were capable of being made more shabby—compounded some hot mixture in a jug with gin and lemons, and stirred it round and round and put it on the hob to simmer; Master Peter, and the two ubiquitous young Cratchits went to fetch the goose, with which they soon returned in high procession.

Such a bustle ensued that you might have thought a goose the rarest of all birds; a feathered phenomenon, to which a black swan was a matter of course—and in truth it was something very like it in that house. Mrs. Cratchit made the gravy (ready beforehand in a little saucepan) hissing hot; Master Peter mashed the potatoes with incredible vigour; Miss Belinda sweetened up the apple-sauce; Martha dusted the hot plates; Bob took Tiny Tim beside him in a tiny corner at the table; the two young Cratchits set chairs for everybody, not forgetting themselves, and mounting guard upon their posts, crammed spoons into their mouths, lest they should shriek for goose before their turn came to be helped. At last the dishes were set on, and grace was said.

It was succeeded by a breathless pause, as Mrs. Cratchit, looking slowly all along the carving-knife, prepared to plunge it in the breast; but when she did, and when the long-expected gush of stuffing issued forth, one murmur of delight arose all round the board, and even Tiny Tim, excited by the two young Cratchits, beat on the table with the handle of his knife, and feebly cried Hurrah!

There never was such a goose. Bob said he didn't believe there ever was such a goose cooked. Its tenderness and flavour, size and cheapness, were the themes of universal admiration. Eked out by apple-sauce and mashed potatoes, it was a sufficient dinner for the whole family; indeed, as Mrs. Cratchit said with great delight (surveying one small atom of a bone upon the dish), they hadn't ate it all at last! Yet every one had had enough, and the youngest Cratchits in particular, were steeped in sage and onion to the eyebrows! But now, the plates being changed by Miss Belinda, Mrs. Cratchit left the room alone—too nervous to bear witnesses—to take the pudding up and bring it in.

Suppose it should not be done enough! Suppose it should break in turning out! Suppose somebody should have got over the wall of the back-yard, and stolen it, while they were merry with the goose—a supposition at which the two young Cratchits became livid! All sorts of horrors were supposed.

Hallo! A great deal of steam! The pudding was out of the copper. A smell like a washing-day! That was the cloth. A smell like an eating-house and a pastrycook's next door to each other, with a laundress's next door to that! That was the pudding! In half a minute Mrs. Cratchit entered—flushed, but smiling proudly—with the pudding, like a speckled cannon-ball, so hard and firm, blazing in half of half-a-quartern of ignited brandy, and bedight with Christmas holly stuck into the top.

Oh, a wonderful pudding! Bob Cratchit said, and calmly too, that he regarded it as the greatest success achieved by Mrs. Cratchit since their marriage. Mrs. Cratchit said that now the weight was off her mind, she would confess she had had her doubts about the quantity of flour. Everybody had something to say about it, but nobody said or thought it was at all a small pudding for a large family. It would have been flat heresy to do so. Any Cratchit would have blushed to hint at such a thing.

At last the dinner was all done, the cloth was cleared, the hearth swept, and the fire made up. The compound in the jug being tasted, and considered perfect, apples and oranges were put upon the table, and a shovelful of chestnuts on the fire. Then all the Cratchit family drew round the hearth, in what Bob Cratchit called a circle, meaning half a one; and at Bob Cratchit's elbow stood the family display of glass. Two tumblers, and a custard-cup without a handle.

These held the hot stuff from the jug, however, as well as golden goblets would have done; and Bob served it out with beaming looks, while the chestnuts on the fire sputtered and cracked noisily. Then Bob proposed:

"A Merry Christmas to us all, my dears. God bless us!"

Which all the family re-echoed.

"God bless us every one!" said Tiny Tim, the last of all.

The Oak of Geismar

by HENRY VAN DYKE

THROUGH the wide forest which rolled over the hills of central Germany, nearly twelve centuries ago, on the day before Christmas, a little company of pilgrims was journeying northward.

At the head of the band was a man about forty years of age, fair and slight, with eyes as blue as the sky and full of kindness, yet flashing with the fire of a will that knew no weakness and no fear. His thick garments of fur were covered with a coarse black robe, girt high about his waist, so that it might not hinder his quick stride; and in his right hand he carried a strong staff, fashioned at the upper end into the semblance of a cross. It was Winfrid of England, who had left his fair patrimony and noble estate in Wessex to bring the Gospel to his heathen kinsmen in the woodland of Thuringia and Hesse.

Close behind him, and keeping step with him like an inseparable companion, was the young Prince Gregor, whose heart Winfrid had won three years before in the cloister of Pfalzel. "Grandmother," cried the lad to the Abbess Addula, the daughter of King Dagobert, "if thou wilt not give me a horse, I will follow my master afoot." And the prince had kept his word. Long journeys through the wilderness had made a man of him in strength as well as in spirit; and now he marched with Winfrid, a sturdy, resolute figure, in woodman's dress, with short cloak and cap of wolf's skin, carrying on his shoulder a mightly axe, to cut away the fallen trees which here and there blocked the way.

Behind these leaders followed a group of foresters and servants; then two sledge-horses blowing thick clouds of steam from their frosty nostrils; and last of all came the rear-guard, armed with bows and javelins. For it was no light adventure, in those days, to pass through the weird woodland, haunted by bear and wolf, lynx and boar, and sheltering in its gloomy recesses men who were fiercer than beasts of prey—outlaws and sturdy robbers and mad were-wolves.

The travellers were surrounded by an ocean of trees, so vast, so full of endless billows, that it seemed to be pressing on every side to overwhelm them. Gnarled oaks, with branches twisted and knotted as if in rage, rose in groves like tidal waves. Smooth forests of beech-trees, round and gray, swept over the knolls and slopes of land in a mighty ground-swell. But most of all, the multitude of pines and firs, innumerable and monotonous, with straight, stark trunks, and branches woven together in an unbroken flood of darkest green, crowded through the valleys and over the hills, rising on the highest ridges into ragged crests, like the foaming edge of breakers. Through this sea of shadows ran a narrow stream of shining whiteness—an ancient Roman road, covered with snow—and along this open track the travellers held their way; heavily, for the drifts were deep; warily, for the hard winter had driven many packs of wolves down from the mountains.

The steps of the pilgrims were noiseless; but the sledges creaked over the dry snow, and the panting of the horses echoed through the still, cold air. The pale-blue shadows on the western side of the road grew longer. The sun, declining through its shallow arch dropped behind the tree-tops. Darkness followed swiftly, as if it had been a bird of prey waiting for this sign to sweep down upon the world.

"Father," said Gregor to the leader, "surely this day's march is done. It is time to rest, and eat, and sleep. If we press onward now, we cannot see our steps; and will not that be against the word of the psalmist David, who bids us not to put confidence in the legs of a man."

Winfrid laughed silently, in the manner of those who have lived long in the woods. "Nay, my son Gregor," said he, "thou hast tripped, even now, upon thy text. For David said only, 'I take no pleasure in the legs of a man.' And so say I, for I am not minded to spare thy legs or mine, until we come farther on our way, and do what must be done this night. Draw thy belt tighter, my son, and hew me out this little fir that bars the road, for our camp-ground is not here."

The youth obeyed; and while two of the foresters sprang to help him, and the soft fir-wood yielded to the stroke of the axes, and the snow flew from the bending branches, Winfrid turned and spoke to his followers in a cheerful voice that refreshed them like wine.

"Courage, brothers, and forward yet a little. God's moon will light us presently, and the path is plain. Well know I that ye are weary; and my own heart wearies also for the home in England, where those I love so dearly are keeping feast this Christmas-eve. Oh, that I might escape from this wild, storm-tossed sea of Germany into the peaceful haven of my fatherland! But we have work to do before we feast to-night. For this is the Yule-tide, and the heathen people of the forest have gathered at the Oak of Geismar to worship their god, Thor; and strange things will be seen there, and deeds which make the soul black. But we are sent to lighten their darkness; and we will teach our kinsmen to keep a Christmas with us such as the woodland has never known. Forward, then, in God's name!"

A murmur of assent came from the men. Even the horses seemed to take fresh heart. They flattened their backs to draw the heavy loads, and blew the frost from their nostrils as they pushed ahead. The night grew broader and less oppressive. A gate of brightness was opened secretly somewhere in the sky; higher and higher swelled the clear moonflood, until it poured over the eastern wall of forest into the road. A drove of wolves howled faintly in the distance, but they were receding, and the sound soon vanished. The stars sparkled merrily through the stringent air; the small, round moon shone like silver; and little breaths of the dreaming wind wandered whispering across the pointed fir-tops, as the pilgrims toiled bravely onward, following their clue of light through a labyrinth of darkness.

After a while the road began to open out a little. There were spaces of meadow-land, fringed with alders, behind which a boisterous river ran, clashing through spears of ice. Rude houses of hewn logs appeared in the openings, each one casting a patch of inky blackness upon the snow. Then the travellers passed a larger group of dwellings, all silent and unlighted; and beyond, they saw a great house, with many outbuildings and enclosed courtyards, from which the hounds bayed furiously, and a noise of stamping horses came from the stalls. But there was no other sound of life. The fields around lay bare to the moon. They saw no man, except once, on a path that skirted the farther edge of a meadow, three dark figures passed them, running very swiftly.

Then the road plunged again into a dense thicket, traversed it, and climbing to the left, emerged suddenly upon a glade, round and level except at the northern side, where a swelling hillock was crowned with a huge oak-tree. It towered above the heath, and stood like a giant with contorted arms, leading on the host of lesser trees. "Here," cried Winfrid, as his eyes flashed and his hand lifted his heavy staff, "here is the Thunder-oak; and here the cross of Christ shall break the hammer of the false god Thor."

In front of the tree a blazing fire of resinous wood sent its tongues of flame and fountains of sparks far up into the sky, and a great throng of people were gathered around it in a half-circle. The aspect of the multitude, seen against that fierce illumination, was like the silhouette of a crowd, black and mysterious. As the travellers left their sledges in the edge of the thicket and crossed the glade, none turned to notice them; all the people were looking intently toward the fire at the foot of the oak.

Then Winfrid's voice rang out. "Hail, ye sons of the forest! A stranger claims the warmth of your fire in the winter night."

Swiftly, and as with a single motion, a thousand eyes were bent upon the speaker. The semicircle opened silently in the middle; Winfrid entered with his followers; it closed again behind them. Then, as they looked round the curving ranks, they saw that the hue of the assemblage was not black, but white—dazzling, radiant, solemn, death-like. White, the robes of the women clustered together at the points of the wide crescent; white, the glittering byrnies of the warriors standing in close ranks; white, the fur mantles of the aged men who held the central place in the circle; white, with the shimmer of silver ornaments and the snowy purity of lamb's-wool, the raiment of a little group of children who stood close by the fire; white in the pallor of awe and fear, the faces of all who looked at them; white as drifts of snow the long beard of the old priest, Hunrad, who advanced to meet the travellers.

"Who are you? Whence come you, and what seek you here?" His voice was heavy and toneless as a muffled bell.

"Your kinsman am I, of the German brotherhood," answered Winfrid, "and from Wessex, beyond the sea, have I come to bring you a greeting from that land, and a message from the All-Father, whose servant I am."

"Welcome, then," said Hunrad, "welcome, kinsman, and be silent; for what passes here is too high to wait, and must be done before the moon crosses the middle heaven, unless indeed, thou hast some sign or token from the gods. Canst thou work miracles?"

The question came sharply, as if a sudden gleam of hope had flashed through the tangle of the old priest's mind. But Winfrid's voice sank lower and a cloud of disappointment passed over his face as he replied: "Nay, miracles have I never wrought, though I have heard of many; but the All-Father has given no power to my hands save such as belongs to common man."

"Stand still, then, thou common man," said Hunrad, scornfully, "and behold what the gods have called us hither to do. This night is the death-night of the sun-god, Baldur the Beautiful, beloved of gods and men. This night is the hour of darkness and the power of winter, of sacrifice and mighty fear. This night the great Thor, the god of thunder and war, to whom this oak is sacred, is grieved for the death of Baldur, and angry with this people because they have forsaken his worship. Long is it since an offering has been laid upon his altar, long since the roots of his holy tree have been fed with blood. Therefore its leaves have withered before the time, and its boughs are heavy with death. Therefore the Slavs and the Saxons have beaten us in battle. Therefore the harvests have failed, and the wolf-hordes have ravaged the folds, and the strength has departed from the bow, and the wood of the spear has broken, and the wild boar has slain the huntsman. Therefore the plague has fallen on your dwellings, and the dead are more than the living in all your villages. Answer me, ye people, are not these things true?"

A hoarse sound of approval ran through the circle. A chant, in which the voices of the men and women blended, like the shrill wind in the pine-trees above the rumbling thunder of a waterfall, rose and fell in rude cadences.

O Thor, the Thunderer,
Mighty and merciless,
Spare us from smiting!
Heave not thy hammer,
Angry, against us;
Plague not thy people.
Take from our treasure
Richest of ransom.
Silver we send thee,
Jewels and javelins,
Goodliest garments,
All our possessions,
Priceless, we proffer.
Sheep will we slaughter,
Steeds will we sacrifice;
Bright blood shall bathe thee,

O tree of Thunder,
Life floods shall lave thee,
Strong wood of wonder.
Mighty, have mercy,
Smite us no more,
Spare us and save us,
Spare us, Thor! Thor!

With two great shouts the song ended, and a stillness followed so intense that the crackling of the fire was heard distinctly. The old priest stood silent for a moment. His shaggy brows swept down over his eyes like snow-drifts quenching flame. Then he lifted his face and spoke.

"None of these things will please the god. More costly is the offering that shall cleanse your sin, more precious the crimson dew that shall send new life into this holy tree of blood. Thor claims your dearest and your noblest gift."

Hunrad moved nearer to the handful of children who stood watching the red mines in the fire and the swarms of spark-serpents darting upward. They had heeded none of the priest's words, and did not notice now that he approached them, so eager were they to see which fiery snake would go highest among the oak branches. Foremost among them, and most intent on the pretty game, was a boy like a sun-ray, slender and quick, with blithe brown eyes and hair of spun silk. The priest's hand was laid upon his shoulder. The boy turned and looked up in his face.

"Here," said the old man, with his voice vibrating as when a thick rope is strained by a ship swinging from her moorings, "here is the chosen one, the eldest son of the Prince, the darling of the people. Hearken, Asulf, wilt thou go to Valhalla, where the heroes dwell with the gods, to bear a message to Thor?"

The boy answered, swift and clear:

"Yes, priest, I will go if my father bids me. Is it far away? Shall I run quickly? Must I take my bow and arrows for the wolves?"

The boy's father, Duke Alvold, standing among his bearded warriors, drew his breath deep, and leaned so heavily on the handle of his spear that the wood cracked. And his wife, Thekla, bending forward from the ranks of women, pushed the golden hair from her forehead with one hand, and with the other dragged at the silver chain about her neck until the rough links pierced her flesh, and the red drops fell unheeded on the snow of her breast. A sigh passed through the crowd, like the murmur of the forest before the storm breaks. Yet no one spoke save Hunrad:

"Yes, my Prince, both bow and spear shalt thou have, for the way is long, and thou art a brave huntsman. But in darkness thou must journey for a little space, and with eyes blindfolded. Fearest thou?"

"Naught fear I," said the boy, "neither darkness, nor the great bear, nor the were-wolf. For I am Alvold's son, and the defender of my folk."

Then the priest led the child in his raiment of lamb's-wool to a broad stone in front of the fire, and gave him his little bow tipped with silver, and his spear with shining head of iron; he bound the child's eyes with a white cloth, and bade him kneel beside the stone with his face to the east. Unconsciously the wide arc of spectators drew inward toward the centre, as the ends of the bow draw together when the cord is stretched. Winfrid moved noiselessly until he stood close behind the priest.

The old man stooped to lift a black hammer of stone from the ground—the sacred hammer of the god Thor.

Summoning all the strength of his withered arms, he swung it high in the air. It poised for an instant above the child's fair head—death cruel and imminent—then turned to fall.

One keen cry shrilled out from where the women stood, "Me! not Asulf!" Winfrid's heavy staff thrust mightily against the hammer's handle as it fell. Sideways it glanced from the old man's grasp, and the black stone, striking on the altar's edge, split in twain. A shout of awe and joy rolled along the living circle; and the branches of the oak shivered; and the flames leaped higher; and as the shout died away the people saw the lady Thekla, with her arms clasped round her child, and above them, on the altar-stone, Winfrid, his face shining like an angel's.

"Hearken, ye sons of the forests! No blood shall flow this night save that which pity has drawn from a mother's breast. For this is the birth-night of the white Christ, the son of the All-Father, the Saviour of mankind. Fairer is he than Baldur the Beautiful, greater than Odin the Wise, kinder than Freya the Good. Since he has come sacrifice is ended. The dark Thor, on whom ye have vainly called, is dead. Deep in the shades of Niffelheim he is lost forever. And now on this Christ-night ye shall begin to live. This Blood-tree shall darken your land no more. In the name of the Lord I will destroy it."

He grasped the broad axe from the hand of Gregor, and striding to the oak began to hew against it. Then the sole wonder in Winfrid's life came to pass. For, as the bright blade circled above his head, and the flakes of wood flew from the deepening gash in the body of the tree, a whirling wind passed over the forest. It gripped the oak from its foundations. Backward it fell like a tower, groaning as it split asunder in four pieces. But just behind it, and unharmed by the ruin, stood a young fir-tree, pointing a green spire toward the stars.

Winfrid let the axe drop, and turned to speak to the people.

"This little tree, a young child of the forest, shall be your holy tree to-night. It is the wood of peace, for your houses are built of the fir. It is the sign of an endless life, for its leaves are ever green. See how it points upward to heaven. Let this be called the tree of the Christ-child; gather about it, not in the wild wood, but in your own homes; there it will shelter no deeds of blood, but loving gifts and rites of kindness."

So they took the fir-tree from its place, and carried it in joyful procession to the edge of the glade, and laid it on one of the sledges. The horse tossed his head and drew bravely at his load, as if the new burden had lightened it. When they came to the village, Alvold bade them open the doors of his great hall and set the tree in the midst of it. They kindled lights among its branches, till it seemed to be tangled full of stars. The children encircled it wondering, and the sweet smell of the balsam filled the house.

Then Winfrid stood up on the dais at the end of the hall, with the old priest sitting at his feet near by, and told the story of Bethlehem, of the babe in the manger, of the shepherds on the hillside, of the host of angels and their strange music. All listened, even the children, charmed into stillness.

But the boy Asulf, on his mother's knees, folded warm by her soft arms, and wondering a little at the stains on her breast, put up his lips to her ear and whispered, "Mother, listen now, for I hear those angels singing again behind the tree."

And some say that it was true; but others say that it was the Prince Gregor and his companions, at the lower end of the hall, softly chanting their Christmas hymn:

All glory be to God on high,
And to the earth be peace;
Good-will, henceforth, from heaven to men
Begin, and never cease.

The Noel Candle

by CLEMENT C. MOORE

IT was Christmas eve in Rheims, nearly five hundred years ago. The great cathedral towered high above the city, its spires seemed to reach to the very skies, and the square in front of the church was thronged with people, celebrating the joyous Noel, the Christmas time. Children darted here and there through the crowd, shrieking with laughter. On one corner a group of well-dressed youths and maidens were dancing to the music of a lute and tambourine; on another a number of boys sang old carols. Others strolled about in groups of two and three, chatting and laughing, while the older and more serious went their way, candle in hand, toward the cathedral, where masses were being chanted in Latin. Though these church-goers were more quiet, it was evident that they were happy, for their faces shone with contentment. It did not seem that there could be, in all the city of Rheims, one sad or lonely heart.

Yet there were four. Three of them dwelt in a squalid hovel by the riverside, a tiny shed or lean-to which stood beside a stable. Though its outward appearance was so dismal, once within the door, one might have been surprised to see how neat and trim it was kept. There was but one room which served at once as living-room, dining-room, bed-room and kitchen for three people. The rough stone floor was carefully swept and polished. In one corner lay a straw-filled mattress, but the covers drawn over it, though patched and darned in a dozen places, were spotlessly clean. A rude table, a broken chair, a stool and a clumsy bench completed the furniture of the room. In a far corner stood a small charcoal brazier, whose feeble fire served not only to cook the meals, but to warm the dwellers in the hut. Some cracked earthen kettles hung beside it.

The one touch of brightness and beauty in the little room was supplied by a tiny shrine, built on a shelf at the rear wall. A few field flowers in a bowl stood before it, and from the edge of the shelf hung a silken sash which once had held a knight's shield. It was of scarlet, heavily embroidered in gold, and bore a devise of a lion, surmounted by the lily of France.

Three people were in the room. A young woman was bending over a small spinning wheel, a boy of seven was setting the table with their few cracked dishes, and a girl a year or so older was leaning over a kettle on the brazier, stirring its contents from time to time. The lady, whose beauty seemed to shine in the poor room, despite her shabby clothing, was Madame la Comtesse Marie de Malincourt, and the boy and girl, her son and daughter, Louis and Jeanne.

As she worked the lady was thinking sadly of that Christmas eve only a year before, when all had been so different. Then she had lived in a great castle, and on the eve of Noel, as she had done for a half dozen years before, she and her husband and the children had gone down to the castle gate to greet the crowd that had assembled. The old, the ailing, and the poor had gathered there, and that meant nearly all the village. Out among the crowd they had gone, followed by a dozen servants, laden down like beasts of burden and to each villager the lady had made gifts of warm clothing, of healing herbs, and of wholesome food. Even Louis and Jeanne, young as they were, had given from their store of toys and baubles to the children of the village.

Then the tide of war had swept over their happy valley; the castle had been attacked, defended, and lost, then sacked and pillaged by the victors. Lady Marie had even seen them lead her husband away a prisoner. She had fled with her children, down a secret passage out into the night and away to the village. She found it deserted, the villagers driven out before the sword.

During the months that had ensued the three had been wanderers along the highway. Bit by bit Lady Marie had given her jewels and trinkets, then those of the children, in exchange for food and lodging. Even her velvet robe, with its soft fur mantle, had gone to the wife of a rich burgher, and the pretty clothing of Louis and Jeanne had long since been replaced with coarse peasant garb. One thing alone remained of all their riches—the cover of her husband's shield, which little Louis had brought from the castle that dreadful night. "Father gave it to me to keep until he came back," he said, and through all the terrors of flight he had clung to it. It was very dear to them all. It seemed a bit of their old life, and a constant reminder of the dear lost father.

"Mother," said Jeanne suddenly, interrupting the current of her mother's sad thoughts, "it is Noel tonight."

"Yes, my child," Lady Marie answered with a sigh, "but there will be no toys, or sweets, or pretty things for thee or little Louis this Noel."

"We want them not," the children answered, almost in unison. "We have thee, dear mother, and we can keep the Noel in our hearts," added Jeanne.

Her mother looked up from the wheel and smiled at her. "Yes, though life is hard," she said, "still, we have each other, and though we are sad, perhaps there are other hearts in Rheims that grieve tonight. I wish I might give, as once I did, to the poor, but I have nothing to give. We have ourselves become the poor." She resumed her work, but there was silence in the room save for the whir of the wheel.

"Mother," Jeanne spoke again excitedly, "I know something we can give." As she talked she caught up the small tallow dip candle from the table and hurried with it to the one window of the hut.

"See," she went on, "I will put it here—on the sill—so—and perhaps someone who passes, someone like ourselves lonely and forlorn, will be the happier for my little gift of light. There—see how it shines out on the snow," and she stood back to survey her work.

"You are a good child, Jeanne," said Lady Marie, then, sighing, she resumed her work, her silence, her sad thoughts.

Down in the great square, among all the lights and gayety, was another sad heart. It beat in the breast of a little lad of nine, a boy whose clothes were shabby and ragged, whose bare feet were thrust into clumsy wooden sabots, and with no covering on his head but his own fair hair. He was utterly alone, without money, without friends, cold, hungry, miserable. When it seemed he could bear this burden alone no longer he tried to tell his story to some of the smiling people he saw about him. Surely among so many he would find friends. But no one took any interest in him, other than to frown at him, or elbow him roughly out of the way, and one man shook him by the shoulder, and called him a beggar.

He left the square at last in utter discouragement, and began to tramp the streets, stopping now and then at splendid dwellings through whose windows streamed bright lights like a welcoming smile. But there was no welcome for the lonely child. Fat, well-dressed servants turned him away with angry words, and threatened him with their dogs.

It was dark in the streets of Rheims now, and the air was growing colder, but the child tramped on, trying desperately to find shelter before the night closed in. At last, far off down by the river, he saw a tiny gleam of light appear suddenly at a window and he hurried toward it. As he neared it, the boy saw that it was only a small tallow dip at the window of a hovel, the poorest and meanest hut in all Rheims, but the steady light of the tiny flame brought a sudden glow to his heart and he ran forward and knocked at the door.

It was opened in an instant by a little girl, and at once the other two in the room had risen to greet him. In another moment he found himself seated on a stool beside the charcoal brazier. The little girl was rubbing one of his cold hands in her two warm palms, while her brother was holding the other, and a beautiful woman, kneeling at his feet, drew off the wooden shoes, and chafed his icy feet. When he was thoroughly warmed, the little girl dished up into three bowls and a cracked cup the stew which had been simmering on the fire. There was only a little of it, a scant meal for themselves, but she passed the fullest bowl to the stranger and made room for him beside her on the bench.

After a word of blessing, they ate their stew, and never had the thin soup tasted so rich or so satisfying to the countess and her children. As they finished, a sudden glowing light filled the room, greater than the brightness of a thousand candles. There was a sound of angel voices, and the stranger child had grown so radiant that they could scarcely bear to look at him.

"Thou, with thy little candle, has lighted the Christ-child on his way to Heaven," said their unknown guest, his hand on the door latch. "This night shall thy dearest wish be granted thee," and in another instant he was gone.

The countess and her children fell on their knees and prayed, and there they still were, almost a quarter of an hour later, when a knight in armor gently pushed open the door and entered the hut.

"Marie! Jeanne! Louis!" he cried in a voice of love and longing. "Do ye not know me after all these weary months of prison and battle, and then of search for thee?"

Immediately his family were clustered about him, and their kisses and embraces were his answer.

"But, father, how did you find us here," cried little Louis at last, when the first raptures of welcome were over.

"A ragged lad I met on the highway told me ye dwelt here," answered the knight.

"The Christ-child," said Lady Marie reverently, and told him the story.

And so, forever after, they and all their descendants, have burned a candle in the window on the eve of Noel, to light the lonely Christ-child on his way.